BLUE HARBOUR REVISITED

Other books by Elizabeth Sharland.

www.sharland.com

Love from Shakespeare to Coward. An anthology

From Shakespeare to Coward

The British on Broadway

A Theatrical Feast. Sugar and Spice in London's Theatreland.

A Theatrical Feast in New York

A Theatrical Feast in Paris

The Best Actress … a theatre novel.

Waiting for Coward … a play.

BARBICAN PRESS
Distributed by Gazelle Services. U.K.

BLUE HARBOUR REVISITED

A GIFT FROM NOËL COWARD

A Theatre Novel

Elizabeth Sharland

iUniverse, Inc.
New York Lincoln Shanghai

BLUE HARBOUR REVISITED
A GIFT FROM NOËL COWARD

iUniverse books may be ordered through booksellers or by contacting:

iUniverse
2021 Pine Lake Road, Suite 100
Lincoln, NE 68512
www.iuniverse.com
1-800-Authors (1-800-288-4677)

Because of the dynamic nature of the Internet, any Web addresses or links contained in this book may have changed since publication and may no longer be valid.

This is a work of fiction. All of the characters, names, incidents, organizations, and dialogue in this novel are either the products of the author's imagination or are used fictitiously.

Sequel to the novel *THE BEST ACTRESS*

ISBN: 978-0-595-45284-2 (pbk)
ISBN: 978-0-595-69335-1 (cloth)
ISBN: 978-0-595-89598-4 (ebk)

Printed in the United States of America

'My dear boy, forget about the motivation. Just say the lines and don't trip over the furniture.'

—Noël Coward.

FOREWORD

When people remember Noël Coward, they immediately associate his name with pleasure, a brilliant wit, a cheerful disposition and they remember his endearing songs, his clever plays, the Coward quotes and his poems. To most of us, who know his works, his name brings a smile and makes the day somehow brighter. His song "I've Been to a Marvellous Party" captures a world which has now disappeared.... the witty, brilliant, elegant figures of a past era. But fortunately we are left with some wonderful interpreters of his work and hopefully they will keep his memory alive.

His philosophy in life included his two well known phrases. "Rise above it ... get on with it." Throughout all the vissitudes of his own life he followed his own advice, and remained a hugely creative force in the theatre and musical worlds. Actors, singers, writers and musicians have a star to guide them, when times are bad and when the show has to go on, they can follow his philosophy.... a true gift, not only to theatre folk but for everyone.

This book is dedicated to the memory of Noël Coward.

ACKNOWLEDGEMENTS

Carl Lennertz (Harper Collins,)John Money, Sandy Paul, John Knowles and the Noël Coward Society, Nan Satter, Corinne Orr, Barbara Cole Folsom (for reading the first drafts,) Gerald and Colman Jones for their constant support, and for everyone at Blue Harbour.

CHAPTER 1

▼

I was just a broken shoelace away from a nervous breakdown. People outside the acting profession really have no idea the level of stress that actors experience. Judi Dench and Helen Mirren could tell you all about it if you don't believe me. So many people let you down. Producers particularly. They treat us like playthings, or puppets in their grand scheme of things. They control your life, your family, your finances, your dreams and that's just for starters. Scratch an actor and he will tell you horror stories. Maybe that's where the term 'scratch and mumble' came from. Yes, we all scratch, and the mumbles are usually rumbles of rage.

My rage is, among other things, over not getting paid yet for my last job and also a review I have just read about Noël Coward. The critic lambastes him for writing plays about silly shallow people, and dismisses his work in one sentence. He obviously can't have seen "In Which We Serve" or "Cavalcade". Even though Coward has been dead for many years he still represents the best of British wit and humour against all odds. Added to that, playing Amanda in "Private Lives" gave me my first big break.

So who is this whippersnapper condemning him? My motto used to be "Carpe diem" but I'd changed it to 'Nil desperandum' meaning of course, "never despair." It usually works for me, but it takes some believing. However you always have people like Coward and Cole Porter as shining examples.

I had come to Cornwall to try to fill my lungs with fresh air after London and dispel the hopelessness I was feeling. Sitting in a country churchyard, my back against an old gravestone, I found myself thinking these grave thoughts. At least I'm still above ground, if only just. I sort of envied the ones who had gone beyond it.

In the past, I'd always gone home, up to Manchester to be with my parents, when I felt like this, but they both had gone now and so was 'home.' I had been a late baby, a surprise, my mother being well over forty. I was the only one, and I lost them early. I still miss them deeply, they were always so supportive, and helped in times like these. They also found solace and fortitude by being Coward devotees, always quoting his outlook on trouble, "Rise above it, get on with it, life goes on!" They were married for over fifty years, so I knew those words must have worked for them and I knew that I needed to heed those words now. They would have said them to me I know.

Two years ago I had won an Oscar for Best Actress. Hollywood was totally overwhelming, particularly on the night itself. Nicole Bennett as best actress had been a dream come true for me. Michael, the love of my life had promised to come over for the big night. We had been living together in London, but instead he had gone off with someone else, married someone else. Unbelievable! I had no idea. The shock was still with me and I had foolishly tried to find him for months afterwards. We had been living together for over a year, I adored him and he had been instrumental in getting me the role. I realized the risk of leaving him to go and film in LA, but he reassured me he would behave himself while I was away. He didn't. The hurt would be in my soul forever,I still dream about him at night. I don't think I will ever recover from it. But you survive these nightmares some-how.

But since then I met Peter who rescued me from the heartbreak about Michael, even though they were friends at one time, he helped me forget that agonizing time.

Also I have two soul mates. Ellen and Charlotte. Ellen is my oldest friend who had been at drama school with me. Charlotte is a young pretty actress who is just starting out in her career. Ellen is a vivacious, chubby, redhead, who sometimes reminds me of Fergie in the way she laughs. She is my support system and we have helped each other over life's hurdles. I couldn't reach her before I left for Cornwall, so I was slightly worried about where she was. She was always working, which is good for an actress, so she was probably off on tour somewhere. Charlotte was a new friend but a real charmer. I needed her right now.

But let me start at the beginning when things were going better.

A year ago, Peter and I had been living in Stratford-upon-Avon for the summer. I was playing lead roles in the company at the Festival Theatre. Portia being one of them, and right now the quality of mercy WAS being strained. But at that time, it was a joy because playing Shakespeare is my idea of heaven. It is always sad to be leaving at the end of a season, so many friends to say goodbye to and so many relationships built up over the summer in the company. It was like a family disbanding. Now that my work was over, we were preparing to move to London. A lot of actors act to forget themselves, so this one of the reasons we hate to be out of work.

It was the first time Peter and I had actually lived together as we both had our own separate flats back in London.

"Do you want to keep all these paperbacks, Nicole?" Peter held up about two dozen in his arms, about to dump them in the bin.

"No, let's leave them for the next tenants, they might like them."

Looking around the room, I knew that the place would look better with some books on the bookshelves. It was almost an empty shell now that we were leaving.

I heaved a battered suitcase from under the bed and started to put more things in it, moving back and forth from the dresser drawers. My hair was a mess. We both looked and felt exhausted. I certainly didn't feel like the Nicole Bennett who was written up as the actress who could play anything from Shakespeare to Coward.

Peter looked so sexy in his old battered blue sweater. I wondered if he still thought I was attractive. A 39 year old, still slender thank goodness, with my blond hair now cut very short, and still curly. But counting every calorie.

"Let's stop for a cup of tea", he said and went into the kitchen.

"I think I'd prefer a gin and tonic, if you don't mind. I know it's early but I'm parched." To hell with the calories this time. This was exceptional work. Moving must be the worst work there is, I thought.

"Moving is like playing Shakespeare", I said. "You never get to sit down unless you are a king".

Smiling at Peter, I still couldn't believe my luck. He was irresistible, a feast for the eyes. His name, Peter Marsh, was well-known in the literary world in London but he looked more like an actor than a writer. He had blond wavy hair, going a tiny bit gray at the sides, tall with blue eyes, with that air of gentleness, which was the first thing that attracted me. His hands were long and sexy, and the way he touched me always gave me a thrill. His legs were sexy too, especially when he wore summer shorts-but then I find most men's legs sexy. I don't know why. Maybe because they never seem to have any horrible cellulite. They're just long, and tanned and strong. I guess that's why I always like acting in costume dramas when the men are dressed in tights. Some of them have gorgeous legs.

I leaned over and switched on the radio. Cole Porter's 'Night and Day' was playing. Why is it that when you hear a piece of music unexpectedly, it can transport you back to another time and place immediately: often hitting you in the pit of your stomach or causing a sudden lump in the throat? Besides reminding me of my mother, who sang it all around the house, hearing it brings back the memory of a moment, or of a person. It usually takes you back to the exact place too. The Beatles' song, 'Yesterday', does the same thing too.

The boxes were piling up. It was hard to move around them.

Peter sat on one of them and observed the mess around us.

"Why don't we just get someone in to help?" I suggested, as I found the gin. I poured two glasses and added tonic and ice. We had been working and packing up since early morning.

"It really is too much for us. Look at all those clothes over the desk!"

"You sound like an old woman, baby!" Peter remarked.

"Baby? Since when did you start calling me baby?"

"Baby. Baby doll. You're 39, I'm fifty so you look like a baby to me."

We sat there discussing what we should throw out and what we should pack until the light outside was gone and we knew we were done for the day.

"I wouldn't mind taking all these plants back with us in the car." I pointed to four of the larger ones in the window.

"You're joking" he said to me as if he had caught me running with a pair of surgical scissors.

"O.K. I'll take some cuttings then." I shrugged.

"Perhaps we shouldn't be moving at all really. Perhaps we should have stayed on here and put some roots down and made it our home." Peter said.

I kissed him.

"Oh yes, those long winter nights would do us in." Already the weather had turned and was bitterly cold. At night, the little cottage was like an igloo. In bed, Peter had completely covered himself up with quilts and blankets. "Besides, the theatre is closed. There is no work here ... That's trouble with the theatre. You have to go where the work is. As a writer, I guess you can work anywhere you want."

"What do you want to do about dinner?" He was getting hungry, I knew the signs.

"Well we can get a take-away if you want but it's a bit too crowded in here. Come on, let's go to the Dirty Duck. Besides we haven't said goodbye to everyone there yet."

Peter shrugged, and put down his glass. "If you like. But last time we were there, I felt there was an unpleasant air of Schadenfreude somehow, even though you said that the theatre still hadn't announced the company for next season."

"No, that's all in your imagination, I know them, they are just all impatient to see if they have been cast, that's all."

We had decided that Peter would move in with me on a return to London and rent out his flat. I couldn't wait.

"I think we should give some dinner parties when we get back. I'd like to invite my old drama teacher, for example, who was so helpful in earlier days." I said. "When you get him going he will talk for hours on end."

"That must be delightful!" smiled Peter, in whose mind nature had unfortunately forgotten to include any capacity whatsoever for becoming passionately interested in methods of acting, either Stanislavski's or others.

Still smiling, he handed me a potato chip.

The gin was making my toes tingle and a sense of well-being and optimism flowed through my body." We had a rather good summer didn't we, all things considered?"

The joy of being in the Warwickshire countryside was almost as great as playing Shakespeare there. Whereas the town of Stratford is overbuilt now, the country around it is picture postcard perfect. The tall trees, the hawthorn hedges, the wild flowers, the old stone walls, and the sunlight casting shadows across the road as you drive along a deserted lane under an archway of trees, everything combines to make it like the magical setting for A Midsummer Night's Dream. But summer is really the only time you would want to be there; you perish in the winter as it is so darn cold. Yesterday we took a picnic down by the river, sitting under a large willow tree, even though it was rather chilly. We spread out our "insalata alla caprese." Slices of red plump, vine-ripened tomatoes, alternating with wedges of creamy mozzarella. But it really didn't taste the same as when eating it in Italy somewhere.

The joy of acting is rather like being able to run along the tops of trees in a forest, lightly stepping on each one. Half flying, half balancing, exciting and dangerous but exhilarating. At last, all your work keeps you afloat as you say the lines and fly, knowing your repetitive practising is kicking in, giving you the ease to do it. Like a concert pianist who suddenly feels his fingers flying, playing every note effortlessly and accurately.

Being with Peter was heaven, after living through Michael's lies and infidelity. I knew I could trust him completely.

"We had a wonderful summer and a fabulous one if they buy my book." He smiled.

Last night in bed he was so restless that neither of us could sleep. He had just mailed off the manuscript yesterday. "It's like the night before you are going into hospital for major surgery" he whispered. "Anything can happen, but there's nothing more you can do. You know you might die under the knife.I suppose getting a rejection letter is better than getting a death certificate, at least you are still around to read it, but after all these months of work, the thought that the book might be killed off so quickly is agonizing. Two years work. You women only take 9 months to give birth and you really don't have to do any work at all, no creative imagination is needed, nature takes care of that. You just go to hospital and suddenly there it is, writers go into the Post Office, stamp their new creation and it is picked up by strangers."

"I know. It must be awful. But your agent isn't a stranger surely."

"No, I mean those guys at the Post Office."

"Ah, yes."

"It's even worse for playwrights. Their baby can die overnight if a critic is in a bad mood, especially in New York."

"I know. I read a novel a few years ago where the young author in total despair, committed suicide after so many rejections, only to have her mother ceaselessly work until she got it published. It was a best seller."

"People with no creativity can't understand the agony of it all. At least actors, artists and composers do. I don't know about editors."

"The good ones do, surely."

I went into the bathroom to freshen up. Looking in the mirror I wondered if I should consider some face work. Not yet. Maybe next year. I stepped on the scales. Well, obviously they were broken, or needed to be adjusted. I couldn't have put on that much! Besides, it was the wrong time of day: you are supposed to weigh yourself early in the morning. I'd think about it tomorrow.

Peter had brought his car around, a super green little Jaguar which he loved, even though he often drove it too fast.

"We could have walked, it's not that far", I said, but I knew he liked to show off the car. It was his pride and joy.

"Watch the ducks!" I said as two of them began to cross the road. They were so tame, they didn't stop for anyone. They really get very cheeky.

Peter quickly swerved.

I began to feel as if this summer would be the one we would remember as one of the best so far. The one where I finally got the parts I wanted on stage and when Peter finished the book he had been working on for years which was a great achievement for both of us.

We finally finished the packing next day and fortunately the sun came out which made the day less sad and as we were leaving we blew a kiss to our little cottage as Peter drove around the bend of the road leading us out of Stratford.

*   *   *   *

Back in London I was restless as I'd ever been. Well that was easy to figure out, I wasn't working that's why. When you hit forty it is very difficult to get work unless you are willing to travel all over the place and do some really stupid stuff. How you appear to yourself is important. Many people judge themselves by what other people think of them … but then they don't know what standards you might have set for yourself and how high your goals may be and how far you fall short of them.

"But maybe your goals are too unrealistic?" Peter asked as he wrapped up the old newspapers to take out the garbage.

"Not to me they aren't. Maybe to others. I am a forty year-old old actress who won an Oscar for one role in a film and now I can't get any work."

"You worked at Stratford."

"That's different. It's classical theatre, which I was trained to do. It's not the same thing."

"Well you keep turning down plays and scripts then you say you can't get any work."

"Yes, I know. But I refuse to do junk. Some of those scripts are so terrible, I can't imagine who would act in them. I want something worthwhile. I wish Tony wouldn't keep sending me such poor material. If you aren't careful and accept something awful, you quickly loose your reputation. After you've reached a certain level, you develop standards. Look at you, you could write potboilers but you don't. You have a reputation and standards too, you know. I know you are trying to write something really good."

"Only since you met you. You are my inspiration."

"And you're gorgeous!" I flung my arms wide then hugged him.

He suddenly said, "I think you'd better marry me."

"Marry you!" I said in mock horror. "You know what they say, don't you? If love is blind, then marriage is an eye-opener!"

"Well we should have had our eyes opened by now, don't you think?"

I looked at him and realized how much I loved him. Not the wild, passionate, animal love but the one that includes loyalty. He hung up my clothes, he put my shoes away, without a comment. I was so untidy and I always begrudged the time having to hang up clothes and clean up.

But all this was quickly ended. Peter died in a car crash two weeks later. He had swerved to miss a dog crossing the road and smashed into the back of a truck.

Does anyone know why these things happen? Does anyone believe it when it does? I had been out all day and when I returned the police were here. It has been so painful and stupid I don't want to think about it. It was an accident, no fault on either side but something that made no sense at all.

I looked in the mirror and my blue eyes were red. Crying always does that. I stepped on the scales and I'd lost five pounds which wasn't surprising as I had no appetite since it all happened. It was like it never happened. I kept waking up thinking that it was all just a bad dream, that everything was normal.

Those first few weeks after his death I try to put out of my mind. Ellen helped tremendously, she took time off and came to stay with me, and came to the funeral with me. She had met Peter several times and really liked him. His mother wanted him to be buried in her local village, near his childhood home, so all that was arranged by her. Although I had never met her she knew we had been living together and obviously his London friends wanted to be there. It was all so sad. She had us for a rather lovely high tea afterwards and I felt sorry I hadn't met her while Peter was alive. She didn't seem upset when the lawyers told her that he had left a sizable amount of money to me. Since I had been working all summer I didn't really need it so I had my manager invest it all for me. At least I owned my own flat, and had managed to save enough to invest some of it.

There is something about grief that only time will heal as the cliché goes … but no one told me about coping with grief in bad weather, which makes it doubly hard. The only thing that I could think about was to go somewhere I had never been before, where there were no memories of Peter or any part of our relationship. The rain and cold were unbearable and the day to day misery of London made me feel that nothing would ever get better.

I used all my resources to clear out his clothes and possessions and now it was as if we had never met. I even put away any photos of him as it still hurt to look at them. The morning I went down to the charity shop with bags of his clothes, I arrived too early as the shop didn't open for another half an hour, so I left the bags by the front door, then went on to buy some groceries. When I walked back, just before they opened, the bags were gone … I guess some homeless person needed them more, and so Peter's blue sweater will be worn by who knows who. I guess I should have kept it in some trunk somewhere and taken it out every now and then to see if I could still sniff him or his after-shave. But there's no practice for this sort of thing.

The memories wouldn't let me alone. Walking in a nearby park, I once again see him pointing out the most lovely row of lilacs trees just before a thunder-storm on a summer evening. Now, when the melodious sky growls like a tawny lion, and everyone is complaining of the storm, it is the memory of Peter that makes me stand alone in ecstasy, inhaling, through the noise of the falling rain, the lingering scent of invisible lilacs. I thought of another song that brought back more memories, one he used to sing, "We'll gather lilacs in the Spring again." Enough. Stop it. Too painful. Walking the streets brought no respite either.

Then one day a few months later, quite by accident, I bumped into Joan Seymour, an actress I had worked with years ago. We recognized each other immediately. I always thought she was rather cold and distant and never very sympathetic: maybe because she was after the same roles I was. We were standing outside a coffee shop, so we agreed to have a quick cup of coffee together to catch up with each other's news. I remembered she was the daughter of a very famous West End actress, Edith Spencer, who had retired about ten years earlier. She had been one of the great Shakespearean actresses, playing all the top roles opposite Laurence Olivier and John Gielgud. Her face and her voice were totally unique. Very tall-almost statuesque—and a beauty, she had conquered the West End many years ago. I remember how I envied Joan her background of wealth and privilege, although I shouldn't have really, because it is all a matter of fate. If you are born into the 'County' set, that fringes on the aristocracy, life can be much more prestigious. Elite private schools are the norm, social and business contacts are already in place, your parents arrange your social life until you're married or in a high powered career, family connections being all important too. But Joan was not a snob, as so many of them are, she managed to carve out her own career, but of course having a famous mother helped. I asked her if Edith was still alive.

"Yes, she is. It's funny you should ask that, because I have just been with her at her flat. She's eighty-five now and we, I mean the family, have decided she will have to give up the flat and go into a retirement home."

"Oh, what a decision to have to make!" I felt very sympathetic, thinking about my own mother … and noticed Joan had become quite warm and much more friendly than in the past.

A little family suffering might have helped.

"Well, actually she doesn't seem to mind at all. Maybe because we have promised her a holiday before the move and that the move will be done while we are away."

"That sounds well done."

I decided not to tell her about my life, or about Peter's death. She hadn't known him, so it wouldn't mean anything to her.

I listened to her planning the trip and talking about why she had given up her career because of her mother's need for her.

"I've really lost touch with many of my old friends, because I was never available when they wanted me to go and see a play, or socialize with them." She was very honest about how stressful it had been for her.

"And how about you?" she asked. "What have you been doing? I saw in the papers that you won an Oscar ... Congratulations ... it was a great film and you were terrific!"

"Thank you. I enjoyed the whole experience but that was ages ago. People forget if you don't follow up immediately with something else."

"I know" she nodded.

Joan broke into my thoughts.

"Mother has always wanted to go to Jamaica. She acted with Noël Coward you know, he asked her many times to go and stay at his house in Jamaica. She never did, because of other commitments, then when he died she thought she would never see the place. Now we hear that the house and the gardens are open to the public, we are going. We looked the house up on the Internet and we have made bookings to stay there." She went on, obviously very keen to go.

"Blue Harbour was his first home there then he built two little villas for his guests to stay in on the property in the garden."

She got up to get the sugar bowl from the next table and I noticed how slim she was. Well-dressed in a bright red wool dress, which matched her coat which she had slung over her chair. She was always very well-groomed, with some kind of pretty piece of jewellery attached to her shoulder or waistline. I envied her appearance, I felt like a drowned rat after the rain, my old khaki raincoat wet and crumpled, and she looked perfectly dry.

Tall, maybe 5 foot 10 with long black hair done up in a bun ... somehow not severe at all but sophisticated as some French women look. I remember she never wore jeans at school, which was amazing. Always some well tailored pair of trousers, or a smart pant suit. Why is that some women have a knack with fashion, they just do.

"You really have a flare for clothes Joan, you always had even at drama school. You look great." I said admiringly.

"Well thank you Nicole, that's a nice compliment. The fact is I'm an impulse buyer, I can't resist going into every dress shop I pass."

I smiled. I certainly could. If it wasn't the prices it was the musak that drove me out. Trying on clothes is stressful enough without having someone screaming at you, which is called singing these days I believe, to entice you to buy. The only impulse buying I did was buying books. After I read a review in a paper, if I liked it and the book sounded interesting I want to read that book straight away! That's one of the joys of living in a big city, you can go and buy a new book the same day as the review comes out. I love the feel of a new book, the crisp clean pages, the glossy cover and the excitement of reading it, often straight through in one go. I wish I could read two books at once.

'Well for me it's books. I love buying books, and reading them immediately. They are usually a lot cheaper than clothes!"

She laughed. We were getting along very well, so finally I told her about Peter and his death.

She reached over and put her hand on mine

"Oh, I'm so sorry Nicole! How terrible."

"The worst is really over now. At least, I think it is. We were living together up in Stratford just before it happened, so I really miss him. We were hoping to get married in December."

We had another coffee and kept talking about all the things we had done since we had last seen each other. Hers was the usual story of auditioning and call backs, then being offered unrewarding roles.

"Sometimes I think producers are just curious. They want to see what I can do, following on after my mother's reputation.I got fed up and stopped going to interviews. It was really unfair, I used to get angry because I am not just a younger version of her. I have my own persona."

We lost track of time. I told her how bored and depressed I was now, reading uninteresting scripts, each week. Suddenly Joan straightened up, leaned over putting her hand on top of mine again.

"I've had an idea, Nicole. Why don't you come out to Jamaica with us? You obviously need a break, you need something to distract you. I'm sure there would be a room for you. Come see Coward's house, shoot the rapids, eat tropical fruits, and drink rum punches on a sultry exotic balcony."

"Well."

"Oh, do say yes! It will be good for you really. You have nothing to lose! You always liked Coward's work so now we can see where he wrote his plays, painted all those wonderful native paintings, and entertained. You know he used to invite all the celebrities to stay with him. Katharine Hepburn loved the place. Marlene Dietrich used to have the smallest villa, and the furniture he bought for her, including an art deco dressing table, is supposed to be still there. Vivien Leigh and Olivier stayed often. People used to visit him from all over the world, including the Queen Mother and Dame Joan Sutherland. Ian Fleming lived just down the road, as well as Errol Flynn. You could probably have the cottage where the Lunts stayed all to yourself. Maybe there are ghosts ... The place must be really rather fabulous!"

"And probably very expensive!"

"No, it really isn't! We were surprised. They include your meals too. But besides the airfare, the hotel I know is not expensive. I'll call you and give you the details and prices. You would be such a great companion, as it is going to be pretty dull with Mum going to bed at 7 p.m. every evening. And then trying to amuse her each day. In fact, I think she would be willing to pay your fare to have you come with us."

"No, I can afford it. Just let me give it some thought."

We finished our coffee, paid the bill then went out into the dark, cold, street. It was beginning to rain again. A taxi sped past and splashed us both. Somehow Joan managed to look chic even with mud dripping off her coat. I just looked bedraggled.

"Goodbye then. I'll call you later."

We shook hands, air kissed again, then opened our umbrellas.

"Bloody hell" I mumbled as I walked straight into the icy wind which blew my umbrella inside out. It was freezing and raining hard. That really made me make up my mind.

'Who needs this?" I said to myself. I realized that there is a better place to be right now, and with friends. Yes, I would go, why not? Nil desperandum. Trying to visualize a tropical landscape, with palm trees, white beaches, sea air, cobalt blue skies was very difficult. There was another world out there, a more sensual world than a wet Charing Cross Road, where it grew dark at 4 p.m. A world where people enjoyed themselves, and were happy to be alive.

"There's got to be something better than this." I waited to cross the road as three No. 38 buses passed by. I felt drained, drained of all feeling except incredible sadness. Then, I guess because we had been talking about him, I heard Coward's words: "Rise above it! Get on with it! Life goes on!"

I had been busy working non-stop, but luckily I was between jobs. Peter's death made me question everything I'd ever thought about life and love and theatre. His death threw me into a tailspin. My priorities were changing. I was still very ambitious but there were other things in life I had missed out on. Travel for pleasure was one of them.

Losing Peter was so painful I wondered if I would ever find lasting love in this lifetime. It would be easier never to open myself to that kind of pain again. I should keep my heart protected so that I won't have to go through such a horrible sense of loss again.

Besides you never really knew if someone wanted to be with you just because you were famous or really liked you for yourself. It makes it hard to embark on any new relationship when you become famous.

I needed to go on this journey, I needed to make a change in my life.

Yes, suddenly I wanted to see where Coward had lived. I had read his diary and knew how much he had loved living in his island retreat.

He sat high on a cliff overlooking the coastline of Jamaica, drinking martinis at dusk, watching the fireflies come out. First he built Blue Harbour, then his little house up the mountain behind it and called it Firefly. Coward then moved out of the main house while his two companions lived down the hill at Blue Harbour. Peter would want me to go I thought. I could hear him saying. "Yes, go and enjoy it."

I phoned Ellen, who was home for once, and told her about meeting Joan and her invitation.

"You must go Nicole, it's so obvious. You always loved Coward and his work. Don't even hesitate! It sounds absolutely lovely."

Later on, the phone rang and it was Joan with all the details. Yes, there is room, she had already phoned the hotel and they could get the same airfare and flights that they had booked. "I think Charlotte might come with us too.", she said.

"Who's Charlotte?"

"Oh, I forgot to tell you. I have a daughter … she is training as an actress, still at drama school … but she wants to come. So we can do things together."

"That sounds like fun!", I said, even though I thought that Charlotte might not fit into the plan to see Noël Coward's house. It would mean nothing to her, as it was a different generation after all.

I spent some time thinking of the equivalent of a person like Coward today. I said to Joan: "Who could you compare Coward to today? Who could Charlotte, the younger generation, compare him to?"

She thought for a minute.

"Stephen Sondheim?" I went on. "Someone who not only writes plays and films then directs them, but acts in them."

"That's a difficult question!" she replied.

"He also wrote dozens of beautiful songs: 'A Room with a View', 'Someday I'll Find You', 'I'll follow my Secret Heart',-and on and on. But the younger generation doesn't know who he is. Maybe Charlotte will be educated by her granny?"

"Neil Simon" springs to mind, but he hasn't written any songs or musicals", said Joan ... "Coward, of course, was also a painter and a celebrity. It is said he was taught to paint by Winston Churchill."

"Just his style! I am looking forward to seeing his studio, where he painted many of his canvases of Jamaica."

A glimpse of Coward's world would do me good. His genius and creativeness were still working when he was sitting in his little house, alone, on top of a mountain, without any outside stimulation, writing his plays and composing songs. I wanted to see his "Room with a view."

CHAPTER 2

▼

Next morning, I went shopping. Not a very good morning. Trying on new swim-suits is my idea of hell. God forbid, is that cellulite on my thighs? Look at yourself in the rear mirror! How can one's body suddenly get so out of control? I hate it. Quick, choose the black suit, one size too big (it might shrink or be a safe-guard for travelling calories). And get out of here. Next, sandals. Not as painful! A straw hat. Sexy sunglasses. Now I felt quite elated and began to enjoy this new activity in expectation of what was to come, my imagination running ahead of me.

Joan's husband was an actor who was currently in a play in the West End, so he couldn't get away, but agreed that Joan should go. Joan's mother would take up one room in the hotel, Joan and her daughter another and I would have the extra room.

We met at Heathrow one week later and we made a strange little group. Lining up at the check-in counter with our tickets and carry-on luggage, I felt as if we were all going off to act in a play somewhere … a new theatre and a new play. Four of us, all women, spanning three generations. Joan looked glamorous in a navy blue dress with white jacket and the usual piece of sparkling jewellery. We were all wondering how it would all go. Smiles all around and a few jokes.

After we had found our seats we sat together in one row. We decided it would be better if we sat on each aisle, so we could change about. The flight was long and uneventful. We dozed, read, chatted and most of all studied the map of Jamaica. The island seemed quite large and we would be going to one part of it that was a long way from the airport. Joan was reading a copy of Coward's diaries which I had brought along … I had read it several times and I knew she would be fascinated with how he found and built his beloved Firefly.

Suddenly the seat belt light went on and there was a terrific jolt when the pilot announced we were entering some turbulent area just before landing. The plane bucketed and pitched before coming in to land. Hot humid air greeted us when we stepped out of the plane. It felt wonderful. There was a calypso band playing when we entered the arrival lounge, and complimentary rum punches with little umbrellas stuck in them. I had two while waiting for our luggage to appear. Gradually my head returned to normal and my spirits lifted, due no doubt to the rum.

When our bags were all stowed, eventually, into a rather battered looking taxi, we started off for Port Maria, and the hotel. The driver was talkative and bothered me because he kept turning around to comment on something taking his eyes off the road. The only trouble is that we couldn't understand his Jamaican accent. Fortunately he didn't ask us many questions, he just kept rattling on about the state of world affairs and about the local customs, his family, his children and we nodded our heads as if we were following him, when we were actually totally lost.

The ride was scenic, enjoyable but very warm and sultry. The driver had the windows open so the hot, perfumed air blew in our faces as we passed by wonderfully flowered trees and bushes, natives walking dangerously close along the roads which had no footpaths or gutters. We passed Ian Fleming's house, Goldeneye, where he had written many of the James Bond books and where he and Coward had partied with Errol Flynn and drank jugs of martinis before driving along to someone's party. God! The road was bad enough when sober, let alone after three martinis!

When the driver pointed out Ian Fleming's house, Edith turned to look and said "I remember meeting Ian in New York. It was in the early days and he was very depressed. His books had been rejected by so many publishers."

"You mean the James Bond stories?"

"Yes. All of them were rejected. He had tried for months and no one was interested. He was totally dejected. It was Coward who made him persist, otherwise he was about to give it all up. He bought this place down here and was ready to retire."

"Can you imagine a world without James Bond? Thank God for Coward! Celia Johnson was married to Ian's brother, Peter. When Coward invited Celia to stay at Blue Harbour, they all became friends. Ian based the character of Bond on his brother who was a British spy." Edith said.

We were fascinated by other stories that she told us. All because they were about such original people. Not only theatre people, who were our favorites, but about novelists, poets, painters and such, the ones who were movers and shakers when things weren't happening for them. This was when Jamaica had not become a huge tourist spot and these kinds of artists were free to roam around the island, eating in local restaurants, shopping at the markets without being recognized. Errol Flynn had his yacht moored nearby, unguarded.

The natives looked cheerful and friendly, waving and smiling at us. The scenery, the beaches, the foreignness of it all. Not manicured like the Bahamas, just wild and primitive without much traffic or tourist buses.

Some time later we suddenly turned off the road and entered a long winding road which then turned into a gravel parking lot and the sign "Blue Harbour" beside the gate.

The warm humid air, perfumed by the tropical trees, flowers and undergrowth, was penetrating my lungs, relaxing me. It was an incredible change from the icy air of London. There was the house, sitting in a forest of trees, with the aquamarine sea in the background. The home of Noël Coward.

We had arrived.

CHAPTER 3

▼

"Mad dogs and Englishmen go out in the midday sun"
—COWARD.

A native boy greeted us with a wide smile. He and the driver took our bags, then led the way down a narrow concrete path, with lush undergrowth on either side, to the house, which was built on the side of a hill. I remember reading that Coward wrote in his diary that one day had been 'concrete laying day' and that the workers had been laying concrete all day, tons of it, putting in steps and little paths around the property and I noticed it was still holding up very well. I counted 96 steps from the swimming pool to Coward's bedroom one morning, but that was the longest trek by far.

We were full of anticipation and excitement, after reading about the place in Coward's diaries and studying photographs, it was almost unreal that we were now here. So many celebrities had been down this little path to the house where no doubt, Coward had been waiting for them. It was like walking down to a rather secret select place where only the really rich, celebrated and world famous had been allowed. The stars of the theatre world. Laurence Olivier, Alec Guinness, Vivien Leigh, all walked down this simple path where curious photographers, journalists and the public were definitely not allowed. Only the privileged few, the intimate friends of 'The Master'.

We were led on to the ground floor of the main house, and Sarah, the owner's wife came out to greet us. It is a simple square house, on two floors, with a wide verandah around each floor, facing out to the sea. Sarah shook hands with us and explained that her husband was away that week on the mainland on a business trip.

"He will be sorry to have missed you" she said smiling at Edith. Evidently, Sarah's father had bought the house after Coward's death.

We were then shown our rooms. I was given the Villa Chico, in the garden, the smallest villa below the main house. This is where Marlene Dietrich and, before her, Katharine Hepburn stayed. The original furniture was still there. I was going to sleep in the same bed. Looking into the large oval mirror on the dressing table, I realized that they would have looked through it too, and seen the ocean reflected in the background. Were they alone or with someone? There were framed photos of them both on the dressing table and bureau, shown taken in this room and out on the small balcony. I found it slightly eerie, with the only sound being the dramatic noise of the crashing waves and the sea, which was so close by. It was as if that sound was the only thing in this cottage that was in the present. There was a kind of silence in the room, as if it were thick with spoken words of past conversations which still hung in the air, and the feeling of past love making.

I went into the little bathroom, which had not been modernized: there was just a wash basin, toilet and shower stall. I pulled back the shower curtain. There were the original ceramic tiles and chrome fixtures which they must have used. Later as I stepped into the shower I smiled as I thought that I was not only following in their footsteps but standing in them.

Through the thick foliage I could see the path to the other villa, where Joan, Edith and Charlotte would be staying. That was the villa where the Oliviers and the Lunts stayed, again with photos to prove it. Talk about reminiscing! I wondered where else one could actually sleep and wake up in such paradise knowing you were experiencing the pleasure that these people had also loved. The view across the bay was astonishing, you could see it from every part of the property.

We were absolutely delighted with the place. I looked out the large picture window that faced the sea. The view was quite incredible. The aquamarine water seemed transparent. There were three very large yachts sailing by, only about a half a mile out, in full sail. The hotel swimming pool, down at the edge of the sea, was visible through the trees, with the deck chairs surrounding it. Palm trees and other flowering trees I didn't know the name of, were everywhere. Exotic looking flowers seem to be growing wild. Tiger Lilies, lilies of all kinds, cocoanut trees, a riot of color everywhere.

Joan knocked on the door and came across the patio into the room to check it out. She also saw the view.

"Yes, we have the same. Isn't this paradise? … I can't believe we are here. Look at the color of that water. I feel I've lost 30 years. I feel like a teenager again! I am being defrosted! All those years of freezing weather have clogged up my very being! Why do we live in London for heaven's sake. When we could have all this?"

I agreed. "It's better than the south of France! No pollution and no traffic."

We examined the rooms, each of which was slightly different. One had a long divan by the window, another with a longer veranda than mine. But all the balconies had two pretty blue and white striped canvas chairs with matching cushions, with a small white table. The striped awnings of the balconies matched the blue and white chairs. There were window boxes full of red flowers and the blue of the sea behind them.

"Let's go for a swim, shall we?" I said as we looked down at the pool. It looked so inviting and the beach was too far away. We would wait to explore it tomorrow. We were all hot and tired so the pool would refresh us.

"It looks so refreshing … let's go while it is still warm enough to bathe."

The water was divine and we wondered why we were the only ones around. Perhaps it was the end of the season, or everybody was still sleeping or doing whatever they do in the tropics.

Charlotte swam several lengths while Joan and I played around in the water and then got out to dry ourselves with the fluffiest white towels that were set by the deck. We watched her, both of us astonished by the energy she had for swimming those laps. Finally she got out, wrapping a towel around herself, she walked over to join us. We talked about her training at drama school and how different the classes were since we were out school. The obvious change was that there were far less restrictions on what they learnt and what technique they were taught.

A young Jamaican boy suddenly appeared and asked if we would like anything. We ordered afternoon tea, and as he went away we giggled as we imagined what he would bring as afternoon tea. We weren't disappointed. We could have been on board the Q.E.2, as there was a plate of little cakes, scones with dishes of jam and cream and a large pot of tea. We thanked him and he smiled a wide smile with bright white teeth that made him look like an ad for Jamaican hospitality.

I studied Charlotte. She pulled off her swimming cap, a halo of lovely brown hair, naturally curly, surrounded her oval face. Blue eyes like her mother, a tiny nose and a long slim body. She was obviously very fond of her mother and her grandmother. She spread thick butter, jam and clotted cream across a scone and I envied her disregard for calories. Joan and I looked at each other and shrugged.

"Those were the days, when we could do that!" I smiled.

Charlotte was brimming with health and vitality. I was pleased she had come with us. She was a sweet, charming girl, she kept us in stitches doing impersonations of various actresses. She had a list of theatre jokes which kept us entertained, probably in the manner Coward's house guests had done.

"So you are going to follow in your grandmother's footsteps, Charlotte, and become a great actress?" I smiled at her.

"Yes, I am. However, Granny had it much easier in her day!" She put down her cup and saucer.

"What do you mean exactly?" I asked.

"Well there wasn't nearly so much competition then. There are hundreds of us now, all trying to compete, even at drama school. It must be the most overcrowded profession in the world. But if you are born to do it, there's nothing else you want to do."

We sat there taking in the view, the garden, the peacefulness and the heat. I felt as if I had been waiting for something like this for a long time. Ever since Peter's death, there had been a kind of tension, a refusal to let go. I felt better, but I missed Peter, imagining how much he would have loved it here. I had made up my mind that I would not dwell on sad things and having Charlotte and Joan around it was difficult to stay with your own thoughts for long. It was a discipline I was still working on. Put the past behind you, think of the future. What good is thinking over the past and what could have been?

Charlotte was so entertaining, we both watched her as she rehearsed lines, playing out a scene between Viola and Olivia in 'Twelfth Night', doing both parts. She had been working on it at drama school. She really did have talent, it was obvious.

"Lady, you are the cruel'st she alive,

If you will lead these graces to the grave,

And leave the world no copy."

She was very interested to hear all about my stay in Hollywood and if I enjoyed making the films out there. She had seen me on television accepting my Oscar and wanted to know all about the experience.

"I can't imagine the tension you must have gone through … sitting there, trapped in your seat, waiting for the big moment. It must be hell. I don't think anyone should go through that." She said she would never go out there. "Besides, they say that the proverbial casting couch is far worse out there. You don't get a job unless you sleep with someone!" She grimaced. I wondered if she were still a virgin. I would hate to have to bring up a daughter in this age. They seem to know so much, and think so differently than our generation. My mind boggled when I read some of the teenagers' exploits in the newspaper. They know far more than we did about sex and sex education.

"But what if you fall in love Charlotte. What then?"

"I'll think about that if it happens", she smiled back at me.

"Usually marriage and children are very difficult to juggle if you are very ambitious." I sounded so pompous I thought.

"I know, Mum has told me the same thing." She smiled.

"And usually if you are in love with a man, you want to have a child. A copy of him. You will want to leave the world a copy, as Viola says. It is only human nature", I said, hoping that she wouldn't think I was too serious.

"'And leave the world no copy!' I wouldn't mind a copy of Hugh Grant" she laughed. 'Don't worry! I don't think I'll ever marry, let alone have children, so I may escape domesticity if I'm careful."

"We all say that", Joan said, as she rubbed in more sunscreen.

"Well then, I'll try to do what Lady Macbeth attempted. "Unsex me here", gestured Charlotte, putting her hands on her crotch.

"Oh please Charlotte, that's enough. We don't need that speech as well." Joan interrupted by shaking out her towel with a crack.

"Oh, I love that speech! It's so dramatic! I love doing it", Charlotte replied, with a shrug.

She was so natural and unspoilt. I hoped that she would never see the more seemy side of show business, or get caught up with dishonest agents or producers. It happens so often and always to the most modest girls. I remembered the sleazy types I had encountered when I first started out. During our stay we became firm friends and I hoped she would confide in me, back in London because sometimes you prefer not talk to your parents in case they over react and start lecturing as mine often did.

The boy came back to take the tray.

"What's your name?" we asked.

"Manuel, but please call me Manny!" He smiled again and we wondered if we should tip him.

"It's all included in the bill," said Joan.

He must have thought our lily white skin was rather odd but was probably used to seeing nearly naked white skin around the pool all the time.

"I hope Granny is having some tea", murmured Charlotte.

"I'm sure she is, I know she will want to have a little sleep afterwards."

We went into the pool again, it took me back to the Bahamas and I thought about the last time I had been there, so long ago. It was another world. Did I have the same body then? It is said your skin is always replenishing itself so maybe I have a completely different skin now. My bones are the same, but I have a different skin. Therefore I am different.

Joan started remembering some of Coward's anecdotes and even though I had heard them all they were new to Charlotte.

"Remember what Noël Coward said when a 'method' actor asked him about the motivation of a scene? he replied, "My dear boy, forget about the motivation. Just say the lines and don't trip over the furniture."

I joined in with the ones I remembered.... "He was so visual too. In 'Relative Values' he describes a woman as" walking across the ballroom as if she were trudging through deep snow.!" I think my favorite one is about the suicide of a critic. News is brought in that a famous critic has just blown his brains out. Coward lifted the slightly uncomfortable silence by saying casually in his clipped tones, "He must have been an incredibly good shot."

"Remind of me of that famous quip he made about Queen Salote when she was in that open carriage going to the Coronation?"I asked Joan.

"Oh yes, Well, she was massive. She was supposed to be descended from cannibals. Coward was watching and as she passed by someone asked who was the little man seated beside her. "That", replied Coward, "is her lunch."

"Ah yes, I remember, but some say David Niven said it."

"It is getting late … let's go and unpack!" I said.

"Come on, let's go. We can talk later."

After I unpacked I took the empty water jug from the dresser and went up to the main house to see if I could find some ice and to fill the jug.

There was no one around at all. I went into the little bar off the lobby and there on a table by the window was a water jug with water in it.

"Good afternoon!" I turned and there was a rather nice man in tennis shorts and top, with white canvas shoes, walking in. Aged about 50 I guessed. Totally stunned, I offered my hand. He was around 6 feet, brown wavy hair, suntanned, with a rather a lined face, and great legs.

"Good afternoon, I'm Nicole … how do you do?"

"Hullo, I'm Nigel Fox". He had a lovely smile. Good teeth too. He could have been straight out of a Coward play.

"You must have arrived earlier by the morning plane …", he said, smiling directly at me. He had a lovely voice too.

"Yes, we did. We came from London. FOUR women! So unfortunately your peace may be shattered." I still held the water jug in my hand.

"Not at all", he smiled … "it will be nice to have the company."

"I am not staying here" he added. He went on to explain that he was a neighbor and looked in from time to time when Sarah's husband was away, to see if she needed any help. "I must tell you that Sarah did tell me that you were coming and of course, Edith is an actress I have admired tremendously for years. I saw everything she played in before she retired. Is her daughter with her?"

"Yes, she is, as well as her granddaughter!"

"Edith is one of the finest British actresses we have ever had … and the most beautiful. She must be 90 now isn't she?"

"I was told she was 85, so that's close."

"I'm dying for a cup of tea … will you join me? … There is a little kettle here behind the bar, where one can make a cup if necessary. Please join me. Obviously Sarah is out."

"Well I've just had some, but all right, I'll join you."

We sat down in the small terrace outside and sipped our tea.

As we talked, perhaps it was tiredness of the journey but I suddenly began to feel apprehensive, as if I had a premonition of something unexplainable, rather eldritch. It shocked me. You know, like someone walking over your grave. I took in a sharp breath. Maybe it had something to do with the heat, the travelling, and my own feelings about where we were sitting … we were probably sitting exactly where Coward would have sat many years ago. It was like night and day. Contrasting my life that had been so dull compared to the world of Coward.

Why then, the anxiety? I just didn't know. I suddenly thought that perhaps we were intruders. That Coward wouldn't have wanted us here. It had been his home after all where he had worked and entertained his friends. But no, he had invited Edith here many times, so now at least she has come and brought her family and a friend so perhaps he wouldn't have minded. He knew her in London after all and he moved in that kind of class. His talent stretching across all classes.

I felt I needed a drink. Yes, a stiff drink is what was needed.

"Do you mind pouring me a gin and tonic. I feel quite done in." I said.

"Not at all, I'll get it for you."

He brought one for himself as well, which made me feel better.

"That's very kind of you."

We sat there watching the sun go down directly over the sea, as we talked of Coward and just how long he stayed here each year.

"The place is better when there are more people here because it is like the old times when Coward was alive and he had lots of guests staying here. It is nice that you all came together. The house feels better too!", he laughed. "What intrigues me about Coward" I said, "was how he managed to cross all the class barriers in England. He came from a working class family, he didn't go to any prestigious schools, his first concern was his mother and how to help her by earning money and preventing her working herself to death."

"I know, she ran their house as a boarding house", he said.

"But then later on of course, his talent, his work, his songs brought him to the attention of the upper classes and show business celebrities. I suppose he never missed an opportunity. In his diaries, he describes how he ended up entertaining most of the members of the Royal family, and he was invited to the great homes of the aristocrats. He was accepted, and loved by them. I find it quite remarkable that his talent and wit overruled their rigid class system."

"Mind you, he added, "his enemies could say that he slept his way to the top!" He grinned. "All those Guard Officers, who befriended him."

"Well everybody who makes it to the big time, is always accused of sleeping their way to the top."

"I suppose they are," he agreed.

"But with Coward, it was his quick wit and talent that charmed everybody, from his lovers to the Queen Mother."

I looked for a ring on his left hand, trying to find out if he was married or not. There wasn't one, which really didn't mean anything either way.

He stood up to go and get another drink. His shoulders and neck were tanned and muscular. He was very attractive and for a moment I wondered about having an affair with him. There is always that time when you have to make that decision. No, it was too soon after Peter's death. When you're younger, you tend not to think about the consequences. But now I am at an age where balance is important and one can't be too serious or too frivolous, and there's this slightly skewed, ever-present vertigo relating to how precarious it all can be. I had made up my mind I wasn't going to fall in love again, that I was going to protect myself carefully from loss and pain.

However I missed the memory of being close to Peter's body and being held by him, sometimes I longed to be held and hugged by someone.

Surely a holiday fling would be safe enough. I was strong enough to handle that.

The gin was being to kick in, making me more philosophical about being here. The choices we make in life sometimes are made for us, they are not choices really. I suddenly wondered why I hadn't had a child. Silly. I knew why, I wanted a career in the theatre. It was so difficult trying to juggle raising a child and being out all the time. I had decided that years ago ... however just then, I felt as if I had done all the wrong things, made all the wrong choices.

For some reason, Nigel was being wonderfully kind. He asked me questions which I usually resent, but with him it was different.

"So are you preparing another role?", he inquired.

"No, not right now", I smiled. "I am, as they say in the business, resting."

He had seen the Hollywood film and we talked about that for awhile.

"This veranda always reminds me of the time when I talked to Coward about his travels. You know, he would suddenly take off and travel when he was feeling down and depressed", he remarked as he looked down at his drink. He moved an ice cube around with the tip of his finger.

"Yes, I know. I've read his diaries." I said. "Did you know him well then?" I was eager to hear anything new about The Master.

"No, not really. By the time we came here he had moved up to Firefly, so it was more difficult to see him. He had already bought his house in Switzerland, so he was over there a good time of the year."

I wanted to ask him some questions too. But in some circles in England, it is still considered to be ill-mannered to ask a new acquaintance "What do you do?"

I was very tempted, as I was curious. However I'd find out by other means. Maybe from Sarah the next day.

"Are you married?" was another one. But it would destroy the delicate frisson between us.

"Or, how come you came to live out here?"

The British reserve came into play.

The sunset was the usual picture postcard one, and the cool breeze was welcome. I looked at my watch.

"It's getting late. Thank you for the drink. I must go and change. It was good to meet you. Will you be at dinner? Perhaps we will see you later?"

He must have caught the look in my eyes.

When he stood up and I saw those legs again, it was then that I made my decision. Carpe diem. I want this man, I want to sleep with him. He is such a dish. Seize the day. Nil desperandum! I had been grieving for Peter, but this man suddenly made me feel alive again. My heart raced as I felt that old familiar feeling rush through my body. I tried to stop myself from blushing. I realized that being here in Coward's house was having a tremendous effect on me. It was Coward who told us all about this feeling, he wrote songs, lyrics which were created here probably on this very veranda, and I was overwhelmed by this sudden jolt of exhuberance. "Life is for living." Coward used to say. I have never had such a feeling, it must be the climate, the air and the long process of grieving, that completely overwhelmed me.

"After dinner, when the moon comes up you get a wonderful view from that point across the bay", he said. "If you like, we could have a nightcap and drive over there tomorrow night. I have to go to some neighbours for dinner tonight, unfortunately."

"Yes, I'd like that. What time?" I tried to sound casual, as if I couldn't care less either way.

"I'll pick you about 9 after dinner."

He put his glass down and picked up his car keys.

We both felt the chemistry as we shook hands.

"I'll see you tomorrow then." Smiling at him as we said goodbye.

He gave me a slow smile, which scattered my senses to the four winds.

CHAPTER 4

▼

"I've Been to a Marvelous Party!"

—Coward

We all got pretty merry at the bar that night before dinner. Edith especially as she was not used to drinking martinis.

"I think I must be a little drunk" she smiled at us. "As long as I don't start to giggle, I'll be all right." She paused, still smiling. "You know, Coward had to teach Laurence Olivier how to stop giggling on stage, when he was a very young actor. It took him months. He would deliberately say things that were outrageous to Larry who was so humiliated, he stopped." She paused again."Which reminds me of when Larry was actually drunk onstage. He and Ralph Richardson were playing in a Shakespeare play and they had been drinking in the pub before the show, however they had too much. When Larry made his entrance, he heard a woman in the front row say, 'He's drunk!' Larry turned to her and said, 'Madam, if you think I'm drunk, wait till you see the Duke of Buckingham!'"

She went on with more funny stories about Coward and another legendary actor, John Gielgud whose faux pas were also legendary.

"But he was a dear dear man. He complained about his agent when he was 92, and said he was not getting him enough work. However when he was in a play, and the prompter whispered the next line to the people onstage, he answered in a loud voice, 'We know the line, but who says it?'"

After dessert we went out onto the verandah where a full moon was just coming up over the ocean. A magical scene. Edith was on a talking jag and kept us entertained with showbiz stories. She was sparkling that night. It was not only the wine, but the joy of being in Coward's house I think and the memories of him and all the people she had worked with of that generation. They made up the golden age of London's West End and we knew that there will never be anything like it again.

She brought up the fact that older actresses are usually ignored now, whereas the young ones are made-up to play older parts, no one considers making-up older actresses to play younger parts. She then recited a speech of Juliet's which astounded us. She was like a young girl. Charlotte was astonished.

"Sarah Bernhardt was old but she still played "St. Joan" and "Hamlet", Mrs. Patrick Campbell was 50 when she created the role of Eliza Doolittle for GBS. It's a pity all the directors go for the young so much, and don't consider someone who maybe at the same age as the character."

We all agreed.

Edith told us about Alec Guinness when he first started at the Old Vic. Evidently he was so broke he went to Lilian Baylis, the famous founder of the theatre to ask for a raise. "It was well known that she was a very religious person and went to mass every morning on her way to work. Well, she was very surprised and told him that they would have to say a little prayer to decide this matter. She then asked him to kneel down with her, which he did, then after a minute or so, she got up saying "I'm sorry dear, but God says no!"

After dinner, Sarah came in to join us for coffee obviously she was delighted that Edith had come to stay. She produced a piece of paper, which she handed to Edith.

'When we came here to look over the house, we were given this copy of a poem that had been found in Coward's typewriter by his companions after his death. We think it is the last thing he wrote. You probably know it. Would I be asking too much if you would read it to us?"

Sarah handed the paper to her. We all looked at Edith, wondering what her reaction would be. She took out her reading glasses and as soon as she looked at it, her face lit up.

"Of course. I know it."

There was an expectant pause as we waited. She began.

Again there was a pause, as Edith took off her glasses. We were all very moved, not only by the poem but by the way Edith had read it.

"It's all so true." She said. "Most of my friends have gone." She paused. "In fact almost all of them. So now I just use a pencil to write down names in my address book, so I can easily erase them."

We thanked Sarah for a lovely dinner and suddenly all of us felt jet-lagged and decided on an early night. We helped Edith to her cottage and said goodnight. Walking back to my little cottage, I was smiling to myself thinking how wonderful it was to be in the company of Edith, whom I had watched and admired onstage in the West End when she was a huge star, and now to be able to be with her here was rather miraculous.

The path was illuminated down to my little cottage in the moonlight, and there were lights on around the house and gardens so it all looked very secure and safe.

The palm trees were rustling in the sea breeze, and as I got into bed, I lay listening to them swaying back and forth, together with the surf pounding below. It was such a strange new sound to listen to, to go to sleep with, after London. I missed Peter desperately, thinking how much he would have loved this place. Perhaps it was just my suggestibility but the room really did seem to have spirits floating around. Friendly ones. I felt I could almost talk to them. I do most of my musing of the day, lying in bed at night, so it was no different that night. I wondered if Katharine Hepburn had slept alone here, and if so, what were her thoughts, probably wishing Spencer Tracy was with her, or what thoughts did Marlene Dietrich have?

After talking to Nigel, I was restless. I really didn't know what to do next. I didn't want to go back to the theatre, it was too frustrating, too depressing, especially in London. Perhaps I could travel, but I would have to have some purpose for it. I finally fell asleep feeling as if I might have gothic dreams about Jamaican witchcraft or ghosts. But they didn't happen.

Next morning, the breakfast buffet was laid out on the patio. Tropical fruits, mango, paw paw, pineapple, all in a lovely display with bread rolls and biscuits of every kind. Pots of tea and coffee and juice at the other end of the table. It was already hot, so we decided to go down to the beach.

After breakfast, we went and collected our swim suits, suntan cream and all the paraphernalia for the morning. Edith came with us and sat in a folding chair under a large umbrella, just out of earshot from us, as she was trying to write.

Lying on the mattresses in the sun, Joan and I retraced our careers, the plays we had done, the people we had worked with. Lots of talk and gossip about other actors, directors, producers, playwrights and who had done what, who had divorced, or died, or separated. My black mood of last night had disappeared, thank goodness and I felt as if this time would never be recaptured.

It was so innocent and pleasant, as if we all needed a break. So many worries just lifted into the tropical air as you felt the sun shining down and the foliage close by, giving a kind of comfort of its own. The trees, the flowers, the palm fronds all surrounding us with their perfume and beauty.

I made a mental note to remember this scene when I was next back in London trudging through a dark, rainy night with a cold wind blowing and dreary scenes in front of me.

"What are you thinking about?" Joan asked.

I told her about my feelings for Nigel.

"Oh yes, I know, he is a handsome bloke. I noticed him myself", she laughed. "He was coming down the front path yesterday afternoon. I thought he was staying here. Did you find out if he was married?"

"No. But I intend to ask Sarah when I have a chance."

"Ho, HO", she winked.

I really didn't want to tell her about Nigel's invitation.

"Well maybe I would be interested, if you aren't!" She laughed.

"Joan! You're not serious."

Then she admitted that she hadn't had sex for over two years. John, her husband was a heavy drinker and after many years of imbibing, he could not perform anymore. Doctors had warned him, but he ignored them. He kept on drinking.

"I was heartbroken, but what can one do … I'm resigned."

"I can't believe that", I looked at her with surprise.

She shrugged. "It was a decision I had to make. It's like standing on a subway station, edging closer and closer to the tracks, and you suddenly get this irrational impulse to fling yourself off the platform and into the path of a speeding train. Life was better with John than without him and I didn't want to betray him, and I didn't want a divorce. I love him so it wasn't worth it." She looked at me with a steady look, she went on … "At my age, I think sex is overrated. I really don't miss it very much at all. I had my passionate period, if you like, and now it's over. Other things are more important now. Like companionship, loyalty and work."

"You sound as if you have forgotten what it's like!" I smiled, turning around to see where Charlotte was. She was in the water watching a tropical bird walking across the sand.

"If you were trying to keep a marriage together you would do the same thing." She started putting on more suntan lotion. Her body was in really good shape. 'How could John not want to make love to her?', I thought. He must be a fool.

"I suppose I would, but don't you remember how good, good sex is?" I wanted to know if she really felt resigned to her fate. Maybe there is a kind of English-woman that does prefer a hot water bottle.

"Yes, I know. But Coward once said that he hated to fall in love. It was too painful and inconvenient. I'm not going to risk falling in love again. If I sleep with someone I always fall in love with them. I know it's stupid, but there you are and it's not fair to John."

"Well he is not being fair to you'.

"You know, Nicole, I really don't care anymore"

"Of course you do. You must. You will become old and wrinkled before your time". I watched her taking her sunglasses off and wiping them. She still was extremely pretty.

"We all have a cross to bear I suppose, and I guess that's mine."

But what a cross! I thought just how many attractive women would accept not having sex anymore. I tried to guess how much weeping and soul searching she must have done, before she had become so resigned. I wonder if it was her upbringing, her breeding that stopped her reeling from depression or hysteria or both.

Suddenly the lunch bell rang from up at the house. A ship's bell to summon the troops from all parts of the property, which I thought was a clever touch.

"I'm amazed I've got such an appetite", Joan said. "I never eat lunch normally."

We walked up to the main house where a lovely buffet was laid out for us on the wide verandah, overlooking the magnificent view with the sound of surf below. There were all kinds of salads, a fresh fruit platter and freshly baked bread in baskets, then Manny brought out the grilled fish. It was so deliciously fresh.

"I caught it and cleaned it this morning" he smiled. Charlotte took a tray down to Edith who wanted to stay on her own little patio. We had left her at her cottage on the way up from the beach.

After lunch Joan and I decided to stay indoors in the shade for awhile, out of the noonday sun. Charlotte went back to the pool. We went inside to the living room to cool off. All around us were framed photos of the guests who had stayed at Blue Harbour when Coward was in residence.I picked up one with him with Marlene Dietrich. She was smiling broadly from under a large sun hat.

"You know there really aren't any stars like her anymore. Who do you know who has the elegance, sophistication and charisma of these kind of women? Looking at more photos of Katharine Hepburn, Mary Martin, Gertie Lawrence. Those days are over. The modern screen stars are all running around in tee shirts and blue jeans. Dietrich must have known Coward when he was in Paris. Remember he worked there for some time and wrote in his diary about all the wonderful soirees he used to attend there."

"I wish I'd had his address book when I went to Paris" laughed Joan.

She took the photo from me and continued talking, while looking at it.

"I read all about his stay there, going to the British Embassy for parties, being entertained by the creme-de-la crème of Paris. Each evening he met fascinating people like Ginette Spanier, Nancy Mitford and all the Brits who were there. Why did I think that I would meet them too?. Shows you how pathetic one's fantasies can be. Like the people who think that having a coffee in the Deux Magots, or a scotch at La Coupole will inspire them to write like Hemingway or Scott Fitzgerald. Even now, generations later!"

"When were you there?"

"Oh ages ago, when I was waiting around looking for work after drama school. I got so fed up with waiting for my agent to call I had to do something. So I decided to go to Paris. I had always wanted to live there and I thought as soon as I do and as soon as I find an apartment, I'll get a call from him. You know, sod's law."

"Yes, I know all about sod."

"I didn't get a call but I managed to get the love of Paris out of my system" she laughed. "Whoever wrote that song "April in Paris" probably never even went there. It was freezing, it rained every day, and I was totally miserable. I couldn't find a flat that I could afford, the prices were astronomical, so I stayed in the cheap hotel I found. I think it was a brothel as there was so much noise at night, coming and goings up the stairs, but then I was so young and innocent it just didn't register with me. I thought "What a lot of travelling salesmen there seem to be staying there.""

"How awful"

"I was determined to stay on. I walked the streets. I went to museums, art galleries, concerts, always alone.

"Did you mind going around on your own?"

"At first it was O.K. but I was used to going to the theatre with fellow drama students back home, but there was none of that there. Paris can be very lonely. I will never forget staring out the window day after day, feeling terribly low. I had been seeing great art, magnificent architecture, fascinating museums and I felt so insignificant."

"I know the feeling."

"All the artists and writers who have worked there and the people who have written about the city make you feel very uncreative."

"I was only there for two weeks, but I felt it too. One day I was up and in heaven, the next day down in the dumps, maybe it's the weather or something.

Maybe it is just loneliness. I always wanted to travel and see the great cities of the world, but you need to be with someone."

"I filled my days going to language school then writing post cards back home telling them everybody what a wonderful time I was having. I was writing post cards instead of writing a novel. I was just so tied up with the mundane things of daily life, keeping warm, finding enough things to keep me busy and trying to pretend that this was really what I wanted to do. Paris is lovely if you are in love, or have a family with you, or even a friend, but to try living there without any reason besides learning French, forget it."

"You must have been rather broke."

"Yes,I was. Then I had bought a big exercise book and was waiting for inspiration to write something. But I guess there is no such thing as inspiration. Somebody said it is all just hard work and application."

"I know. That's what fascinated me about Coward. I wonder if he believed in it? Remember that story about when he had been working all day, or maybe it was all one weekend, trying to compose a song for one of his shows. He had been at the piano all day and nothing came.… no melody, no words, then he finally got up to go to bed and at the door, he saw he'd left the lamp on at the piano. As he went back to switch it off, suddenly it happened and the melody and words came to him in a flash and he sat down and wrote 'I'll See You Again" straight off."

"Yes, I remember."

"So he had been working all day. It was application and hard work, not inspiration."

"However he did have an inborn talent, as we all know."

"I only know that I tried really hard in Paris and nothing came."

"Well you probably didn't have the right atmosphere or any emotional support."

"I tried. I thought perhaps I should take a lover, but I couldn't find one.

"And yet people still go there and put up with the rudeness and indifference of the French waiters and taxi drivers as well as being overcharged everywhere."

We put down the framed photographs gently as if we were saying goodbye to some wonderful women, the like of whom we will never see again. But then even they probably wouldn't travel with 33 pieces of Vuitton luggage, three furs coats and six hat boxes anymore. Not in this day and age.

"Joan, let's go down for another swim. Shall we?"

"Why not? It's becoming too hot in here."

We went back down to the pool. How refreshing it was, the perfume from the flowers, the smell of the suntan oil and the tropical trees, all around us giving us some semblance of shade. The ocean air was so warm and humid, it penetrated your skin and felt wonderful. We both felt were living this day, at least, as those glamorous stars must have done. The ambience was still there, nothing had changed.

I was half hoping that Nigel might drop by. It would be good to take another look at him before meeting him tonight, after dark, if you know what I mean. I would have liked to chat by the pool to find out more about him. But no such luck although I kept looking up to the verandah in case he was there. I wondered if there was anything going on with him and Sarah but no, he wouldn't have asked me out I felt sure, if he was involved with her. Maybe he was like that Greek chap in the Shirley Valentine movie. Each week he'd drop by, after last week's guests were gone, and case over the new crop of arrivals to take out on his boat, with the same seductive story.

Soaking up the hot sun, my body now totally relaxed, I was torn between wanting to be swept off my feet, to fall head over heels in love with a wildly romantic man or to stay sane, level headed, in charge of my emotions and there-fore my life with no pain, no anguish just a calm orderly life. Well, after my deci-sion of yesterday, I thought I could handle a little holiday romance without any complications. That's what I had made up my mind to do. I thought that Peter would understand."

"You're deep in thought" Joan broke into my musings.

"Oh sorry. I was just thinking about my love life."

"Aren't we all? It's amazing how much time we waste thinking about it."

"Why is it such a hit and miss kind of situation. Some people find their life partner, just like that and live happily ever after, others have a terrible time."

I really didn't want to discuss it anymore. I was still hurting.

The whole day was spent in a kind of haze, of sun, and shade and the wonder-fully refreshing sea. It was a world of bright colors, tropical birds calling around us as well as some squawking ones which we couldn't see.

Later we were woken by Charlotte who had been over to the beach. She had binoculars and was watching the parrots.

"Look at the parrot over there in that tree. Isn't it absolutely gorgeous?"

We watched as it flew off and dived into another tree further away.

"I wonder if we should buy a bird book to find out what species these birds are. Dad would know of course. He has lots of book on birds. He knows so much about everything really."

It was obvious that she adored her father. Joan had done a good job in hiding his faults from her. I thought how good of her, as I remembered how I adored my father too. Mum never criticized him, at least not in front of me. I hoped that John would never let Charlotte down, destroying that love, or that Charlotte would let him down as he must think the world of her. Funny how some kids respect their parents and some don't, even though they were probably treated in much the same way.

"Maybe Sarah has a book somewhere." I wanted to talk to Sarah about Nigel but she wasn't around when we came onto the verandah. Later we had tea around the pool, we decided we would go to Coward's house the next day. The little house he built for himself later on.

Edith was writing her memoirs to give herself something to do while we were there. She kept asking Joan for dates, names of plays, producers,directors, theatres that she had been in. It provided a sentimental touch to each day as we remembered some of the great actors she had worked with in the earlier part of the century.

"How we worked! We toured all over England, you know. Sometimes in the freezing winter there was no heat in the theatre at all. It was unbelievable. I can't think how we stood it really, especially during the war."

Joan remembered her mother being away most of the time and when she was evacuated she didn't see her mother at all.

We talked about the war, and the Blitz and how the theatre people kept on going even through the air raids.

"Charlotte, if an air raid was going on outside, would you stay and sit in the theatre?" I asked.

"I think so", she said "because it would be safer than walking the streets and being hit by flying debris."

I wondered if any theatre had been hit during an air raid and if so which one, what was the play, and was anyone killed. I suppose I would rather be watching a Noël Coward play than a Osborne play, that's for sure, it would be a great deal more entertaining ...

Next morning Manny drove us up to Firefly. He stopped the car just at the beginning of the driveway. We walked up to the house and suddenly heard music. One of the staff had put a record player on, and put on Coward singing his songs. The little studio had been turned into a tiny sound and light projection room and we watched a short film on Coward. Then we were shown his studio where he did most of his painting. He and Cole Lesley would sometimes paint in the nude when it was very hot, so the staff would have to warn them if visitors suddenly arrived unannounced.

The house is very small. Going up a few steps into the house you enter the living room, where Coward's two pianos stand side by side, as well as some of the other original furniture. Off this room, down a few steps, was the very simple kitchen where Coward loved to cook.

There was a framed photo of the Queen Mother, Queen Elizabeth arriving at Firefly. When she visited Jamaica, she made a side trip from Kingston, over the mountains, to have lunch with Coward. He had made a lobster mousse and frozen it, but on the day she arrived it wouldn't defrost. He wrote in his diary, "It had the consistency of Slazenger tennis balls." Panic striken he had to create another dish at the last minute. However, evidently, she had a great time and stayed for three hours.

We went up to the second level of the house, to a lovely open veranda where the view is sensational. From the veranda you enter his bedroom, a simple room, with a small bathroom and shower stall next to it. I was pleased that we were the only visitors that morning so we could take our time. We sat on the sofa on the veranda and looked out across the coastline of Jamaica. The house was right at the top of the hill so there were no other houses around us. It was totally secluded. Later on we walked down to his grave a short distance away where he lies in his favorite place where at the end of the day, they would drink martinis and watch the fireflies come out together with the Jamaican shoreline in the background.

It was so romantic that the staff member who showed us around had tears in her eyes as if it was the first time she had shown the place to visitors. Perhaps she was picking up the vibes that Edith must have been a close friend of Coward's which she was of course and she missed him. How great it must have been to be here with him when he was having a cocktail telling you, perhaps, about the work he had done that day, as he often did to his two faithful companions, Graham and Cole. We walked back to the house and studied some of his paintings and photographs that were still there.

The time flew by, we were still sitting there an hour later when we heard a car drive up, so we knew our peace would be shattered. When a group arrived, we slipped away.

As we drove back down the hill, I thought of the great discipline Coward must have had to keep working in such a remote place. The heat, the mosquitoes, the humidity didn't seem to bother him. But to keep the creative energies going so far away from the lights of Broadway or the West End is remarkable. Of course he always had visitors so they would stimulate him with news and gossip, but to write everyday in that tiny house was something to be wondered at. I was very impressed. His typewriter was still on the desk with a page of dialogue stuck in it.

It had been a memorable afternoon and we were all quite silent in the car. Deep in our own thoughts. Edith broke the silence by some of the remarks she remembered that Coward had made about his house. How excited he had been when he discovered the land and subsequently bought it from a Blanche Black-well, a Jamaican. She spoke of the time when he said he was building his own lit-tle place away from the Blue Harbour, so he could be alone away from the numerous house guests. Like Somerset Maugham, he secluded himself to work every morning. Or like George Bernard Shaw in his study. I went on a pilgrimage to his house in Ayot St.Lawrence when I was rehearsing one of his plays. It is a freezing cold house, ugly and bare. No usual comforts. His dining room was Spartan and I couldn't imagine how he survived in such a bleak house. No warm liquor or wine to keep him warm, or hot roasts either, as he was a teetotaller and a vegetarian. I doubt if Coward would approve, even though he wrote to him early on in his career to ask his advice about a play he had written.

Where did he find solace? In his work.

We drove back to the hotel, we were all very hot and our clothes were sticking to our bodies. So we went in to change for dinner. There was a sound of well-behaved laughter coming from the lounge, Sarah had told us that there were more people coming today.

The day had been so interesting and enjoyable I wondered if the others felt the same let down.

As I went down to the lounge, I heard a man's voice and immediately recognized it even if I couldn't put a name to it. I couldn't imagine who it was. Suddenly Sarah came out of the bar and turned to me.

"Nicole, come in I was just going to fetch you. Someone here knows you."

She led me into the bar and of course I recognized an actor I had worked with about ten years previously. It was Brian Bailey.

Chapter 5

▼

"Brian! What a surprise! I heard your voice in the hall." I walked towards him.

"Darling Nicole! What on earth are you doing here?"

He put down his drink and embraced me. Then two quick air kisses on each side of my face. "It's been ages!" he said, smiling warmly and obviously pleased to see me.

I was impressed. However he didn't look well.

It had been ten years at least. Ten years since Manchester. What a contrast … from Manchester to Jamaica.

"How time flies!" smiling at him.

It seemed that Brian had left the theatre shortly after that. He became a journalist and in time got into specializing in travel. He had written two travel books and was working on a third.

"I bet I know why you are here", I smiled. "You are writing an article about Coward!" I laughed.

"Exactly! So I came to see his house."

"So did we!"

He then looked over and saw Edith walking down to her villa. He was amazed and quickly looked back at me for confirmation, I nodded. He recognized her immediately.

"I came with her and her daughter, who brought her daughter. Did you ever work with Joan Seymour?" I asked him.

"No, but I would have liked to. Can we all sit together at dinner?"

"Of course. They will be interested to meet you, I'm sure."

Again at dinner Edith was the life of the party. Brian was delighted with her anecdotes and we all let her hold the floor particularly as she was enjoying herself so much. Then, over the cheese and biscuits, Edith turned to Brian and asked him what he did. He told her he had been an actor and named some of the companies he had worked in. She looked blank, obviously dismissing him and his work. Maybe it was her age, but it was very clear she wasn't impressed with him at all. He told her he had written plays, then, of course it was rather awkward when she asked him, quite naturally, who had produced them.

"Well I haven't had one professionally produced as yet." he said.

Oh hell, I thought, why did she have to ask that question.

Suddenly he knocked over his full glass of red wine right across the table, on the white linen table cloth.

"Ooops!" I said, rather lamely. Anyone could have done the same thing, but the timing was so unfortunate, he was the centre of attention at that moment. Quickly we tried to mop it up, but we only had the matching white linen napkins at hand, which we really didn't want to use. It made a terrible mess and Brian was overcome with embarrassment, as well as humiliated. We tried to joke about it and my quip of "Brian, I just can't take you anywhere!" fell a bit flat. Not only was he embarrassed but also devastated by Edith's easy dismissal. She wasn't really being unkind, just uninterested, as obviously she didn't know anything about him. Manny came to the rescue, he quickly mopped up the wine and laid a smaller cloth over the stain. We tried to pick up the conversation by reverting back to Edith's career, which we hoped would help Brian's over his uneasiness.

We stayed on for another few minutes, then Brian and I excused ourselves and we went down to sit by the pool as we wanted some time alone, to catch up on old friends.

It was obvious that Brian had been fascinated by Edith but very upset about what had happened at dinner.

"Please Brian don't go on about it. It was an accident, it could have happened to any of us. Let's forget it and talk about something else. If you like I'll spill mine tomorrow if it will make you feel any better."

"All right. I know I'm being a bore."

I knew he wasn't so upset about the spilt wine but rather by the fact that Edith had dismissed him and his work so lightly. Not maliciously but it was just that she didn't know him at all. How deeply upset, I didn't realize till later.

We looked up at the sky. No moon yet, but the stars were like pinholes of light in the dark sky.

We sat in silence for awhile. For once I was at a loss for words.

"You know they gave me Coward's bedroom … up on the top floor. I am overwhelmed!" said Brian. "I have his old bed, and facing the sea. The old desk is still there too, the wooden window shutters, and the big fan over the bed which looks like the original. I never expected to sleep in his room in his bed."

"How lovely", I said. "Can I come up and see?"

"Of course." We went up the stairs and through the only other room on the top floor, which was also a bedroom obviously used by his companion at the time. He quoted Coward as we walked in the door. 'Let's face it, quite a lot has happened in this room over the years."

It was quite eerie then, going into the room which had a simple bare painted wood floor, a four-posted bed, the large tropical fan slowly moving above it, and another door opening out onto the large veranda, which ran around the house. There, suddenly, was the full moon and the moonlight was coming across the sea. The surf was quite high and you could hear the waves even louder up here. To break the silence I said,

"I read somewhere that one of Coward's guests, suddenly burst in to the lounge one morning saying he had to leave, he just couldn't stand the sound of the sea any longer. It was driving him mad."

We went out and stood on the veranda. The whole property was lit up by moonlight. The moon had come up very quickly.

"I remember you wanted to become a playwright when we were working in Manchester", I reminded him. "You would always go straight home, and never to the pub with us, after a show, because you said that was the only time you had to write. Do you remember?"

"Yes, of course I do. I started plays but never finished them. I never seem to have the time. Remember, we were doing one play a week in those days."

"We used to call you a 'right little Noël Coward'! You were disgusted with us!" I laughed.

I could see he was suffering by my conversation. I had touched a nerve, this was something he did not want to talk about.

"I did finish one about a year ago, but my agent hasn't had any luck with it. It has bounced back from producers faster than a tennis ball. Believe me it is all about casting … if I could only get to the people I want."

It was obvious that he was upset, so I changed the subject and talked about his journeys.

"You must have been to some interesting places … I remember you loved the Italian Lakes."

"Yes, I wrote a book about them. I'll send you a copy if you like."

"I'd love that. I want to go there sometime."

"Travel was a godsend for me."

"How do you mean." I asked.

"I don't know about you Nicole, but so many of my very dearest, closest friends have died. People I really loved and admired. They not only inspired me, but life was such fun when they were around. I lost three in one year. It was then I started to travel, because I didn't know what to do. They were gone and I knew I would never meet be able to meet the same kind of people again. They were unique, and I missed them so."

I didn't want to argue with him, or reassure him that maybe he might meet some other equally wonderful people.

It wasn't the time. Nor was I going to make things more miserable by telling him about Peter's death.

Suddenly again, a strange anxiety passed through my body, a sinking feeling, hard to describe. I wondered if it could still be jet lag, it was so overpowering, I took a deep breath.

"Let's have another drink, shall we?" I asked.

Why not? He was sensing my mood, I think.

We went back downstairs, to sit outside the living room on the open veranda. We were alone, as the others had gone back to their villas. He fixed the drinks, and came over and sat down.

He pulled off his jacket, and said quite softly, "You know when I was shown into Coward's old room earlier and was left alone, before dinner, I stood there in the silence. It suddenly came to me. It was an epiphany. It ignited all my senses and left me feeling as though I could fly like some eagle. The drawback was that, like any powerful drug, there were after effects. It took some time for the feeling of intense arousal to evaporate from my bloodstream. My whole life seems so insignificant ... all the things that were really important to me have slipped through my fingers as if I hadn't been aware of what I should have been doing at a certain part of my life. My schooling was all wrong, my activities were the wrong kind compared to what I should have been doing. It is like this air, this rarified air has suddenly cleared my brain. I suddenly see things as they really are, and see how little I have achieved. So much time gone, so much wasted time. The reality is that I am mediocre. I have no talent whatsoever. Even if I had been Coward's companion, for example, I would have botched the job because of my own stupidity. Then of course, Edith put the cap on it, this evening. I feel such a fool. I have spent most of my life in and around the theatre, I love it, but like hundreds of others, I expect, we are little nobodies. Our work means nothing."

"Brian, that's not true. You just don't know what kind of contribution you might have made. Inspired somebody in the audience, a child perhaps, to read Shakespeare or to travel or fulfil their dreams in some way." Of course what he was saying was true. The reaction Brian felt was normal. He had met someone who had been at the top of her profession. Like a young pianist put on the stage at Carnegie Hall and asked to perform for Rubinstein, or a dancer meeting Balanchine, face to face, the reality of your work comes into immediate focus against these celebrated people so you can quickly see how you measure up.

"I guess I never got that 'big break' that's what we are really talking about. When suddenly the whole world changes and your career takes off, when you become "somebody" and people remember your name, and everything is different, and your self confidence soars. Tell me Nicole, how did you get your big break? How did you go on to win that award? Last time we were together it was in the dinky rep company after all." he turned to me looking at me as if he really had to know.

"Well you know what they say, it is all a matter of luck or being at the right place at the right time. You know I was living with Michael, and it was his screenplay that did it. I begged him to let me play the lead role, so eventually they gave it to me at his insistence. However as you probably read in the papers, he dropped me after I went to L.A.to film it. He married someone else, and I lost the love of my life by winning that award. I should write a book called "What Price Hollywood?" Why is it that fame always comes with a price? I don't know if it was worth the agony."

"Of course it was. Otherwise you would still be like me. Unknown and poor."

"Does fame mean that much to you?"

"Is the Pope Catholic?" I want someone like Edith to know who I am, and compliment me on my work."

I suddenly realized that he didn't want to be able to write like Noël Coward. He wanted to BE Noël Coward.

He had been drinking at dinner so he was probably slightly drunk by this time and I wondered what I could do to cheer him up.

"Maybe you will meet someone who will change your life?"

He smiled. "Not at my time of life … Who would be interested?"

"Lots of people. There are a lot of lovely people out there who would like to meet you." I lied. He was not handsome at all, a rugged type with a rather large bulbous nose, short, he'd been a character actor in our company.

He knew that I was lying.

"I know I won't achieve anything much … it is the reality of my life. I don't know why I keep trying. I seem to have lost that drive which is needed at all times."

He was definitely getting drunk. I looked at my watch, it was a few minutes after nine o'clock. I had no idea we had been talking for so long. I stood up and said we should both pack it in.

"Let's talk more tomorrow and maybe we can work on it." I knew he wanted to talk longer but I didn't want to keep Nigel waiting. My heart was jumping with excitement.

Brian looked so upset. He was white as a sheet and began to cry.

"Why didn't God give me the talent, or the breaks, Nicole? Tell me that?" He pulled a hip flask out of his pocket and drank from it.

I had seen enough actors drunk in my time, so this was nothing new.

Usually they were happy drunks, but Brian was obviously very depressed. He would get more maudlin the longer I stayed with him. The sooner he got to bed and slept it off the better.

"Go to bed Brian. You'll feel better in the morning. You've got jetlag. I really have to go now." I gave him a quick peck on the cheek and ran up the steps, around the house, to the parking lot.

I was five minutes late, but Nigel was sitting listening to the car radio and didn't seem to mind.

"Sorry I'm late." I got in the car beside him.

"Not at all. I've only just arrived myself" he looked across at me with that wonderful smile again.

As we drove along the twisting road, we started talking about general things, I was still upset about leaving Brian so abruptly, but I always lose patience when someone is getting drunk. I took a few deep breaths trying hard to calm down, to lighten up. It was actually very enjoyable driving along sitting beside him, a handsome man, in a nice car, with the moon above, it reminded me of sitting beside Peter, or my father when I was little. I concentrated on Nigel, he was a good driver. He was in charge but he was giving me his full attention. Instinctively we both refrained from asking questions about each other's personal life. It was as if we were deliberately avoiding doing so. I didn't want to know about him just then, and I hope he didn't want to know about me. I was still swept away about being at Blue Harbour and wanted to see if he admired Coward as much as I did. At least we were neutral ground. Then I told him about Brian's reaction to sleeping in Coward's room. How he had been in actor but given it up several years ago. I wanted to see how he would react about Brian's anguish. It all came out in a rush as I knew that I wanted him to know. He listened and seemed quite interested, even though most people don't usually have much sympathy or interest in actors and their lives or their problems unless there is one in their immediate family.

"Brian was right. He really hasn't achieved very much with his life ... he adored Coward of course and I wondered if the thought of how much Coward had achieved was depressing him. It was especially real being in Coward's room and knowing how much Coward had achieved-not only his writing, but to be able to build this house and keep a staff, as well as entertaining all his guests."

"Go on", said Nigel as we narrowly missed a local taxi speeding around a bend.

"Many people put their savings into a mutual funds, or securities of some kind. Coward instead spent his money doing wild, creative things. You're not a writer are you?"

"No, I'm not," Nigel laughed. "What has that got to do with it?" He turned and smiled at me.

"Please keep your eyes on the road! How many writers, if they had the money, would go off and build a home, or rather two homes, in a far-off tropical island? Would any of us do that now? I'm absolutely astonished at that side of Coward. Even with all the new kinds of instant communications, which they didn't have in those days. How did he find efficient local tradesmen, buy the land, and leave them to get on with it? What about permits? Who would get those?"

"I don't know, we bought our place fully built", replied Nigel.

"What courage to be such an adventurer, conducting business with laborers, and being prepared for all kinds of emergencies. So what if he came out of his study after composing a song, a legendary song no less? He had to order more concrete. It was just another part of his day. Of course, he did have two competent assistants to help him with the day to day activities. Lots of writers go abroad to live, but don't take on the job of actually building their own place, especially while they are writing and composing."

"He did have help, he had two companions who were with him." Nigel replied.

"I know, but he was the instigator. Not only was he talented in the theatre, but he was also an adventurer."

Nigel pulled up the car in a small car park just by the point near the village. I wondered if he was going to make a pass at me ... The water was so calm and romantic. The moonlight lit up the whole scene almost as if it were day.

We watched a group of fishermen walking up the beach, some had beer bottles in the hands, and they obviously had been drinking. They turned when they saw us stop, and started walking towards the car even though they were several hundred feet away.

"I think it would be better if we moved on", said Nigel, as he started the car again and slowly backed out.

"They maybe harmless enough, but they may have been drinking quite a lot."

He turned the car and headed back until we had nearly reached the hotel.

"Would you like a nightcap at my place? We are just coming up to it? I'd like you to see my place." He put his hand on my knee.

"Yes, I'd like that. I can see your house looks very nice."

When we got into the house, he turned on the several lamps in the living room, which was a long low stone flagged room with very Liberty type furniture. Chintz covered arm chairs and a grandfather clock in the corner. There were lots of books everywhere and a grand piano by the window.

"No questions", I said to myself. Obviously he lives here alone.

He came over and kissed me.

Something inside me that had been very cold and alone for a long time blossomed as though struck by sunlight. Joy sang through me. I wrapped my arms around his neck and returned his kiss with all the passion and love I had been storing up for the right man. He picked me up and carried me into the bed room. I had never experienced such passion as he had. He was so gentle but at the same time so powerful. We both felt a tremendous affection for each other coupled with the wild ecstasy of love-making. He must have been one of the best lovers I ever had and I will never forget how he made me feel so young and vibrant again.

Later on, I finally looked at my watch and realized it would be embarrassing not to be there for breakfast next morning, so with reluctance I got Nigel to drive me back. Thank goodness there were no dogs on the property, or they would have woken everyone up.

We kissed once more before I went through the foyer, to take the little path down to my cottage.

I had a smile on my face and I imagined Nigel had one too. I slept immediately.

CHAPTER 6

───────────▼───────────

Next morning, while lying in bed thinking about our love-making the night before, I heard footsteps hurrying down the path. There was a knock on my door. I got out of bed and slid into my robe. When I opened the door, it was Sarah, who looked terrible.

I knew it must be bad news. "What's wrong?" I asked.

"I'm so sorry, but would you mind staying in your room for half an hour or so…. and not coming up to the house just yet?"

"What's wrong?" I asked again.

"I'm really sorry … but there has been an accident. The police have been called. One of the guests has died. The police have to take out the body so please can you stay in your room for half and hour so."

"You mean Brian?"

"Yes, Brian." She seemed surprised that I would have guessed. "The maid went in to deliver his tray and found him."

"Oh dear … what happened?"

"There was a note, so we presume there was no foul play. He took an overdose it seems."

"Oh God no!" I cried … I felt sick and full of anguish.

"Just give us 30 minutes. I'm so sorry. I know he was a friend of yours" she said.

"More than that, we worked together years ago."

The door closed and I fell onto the bed.

"Oh no! Oh God! Oh no! Poor dear, dear, Brian. How terrible!"

Guilt flooded through my body, like a sharp pain. I rocked back and forth, trying not to cry out loud. "Oh God … poor Brian." My whole body was hurting. "Oh Brian, why did you do it? "I tried walking up and down to ease the pain, but there was more relief just rocking back and forth on the bed.

He had wanted to go on talking, he had wanted to express his anguish, his disappointments, his failures last night and I had cut him off to go and meet Nigel. I had heard dozens of actors go on about their disappointments so many times, drunk and sober, but this time I should have realized the depth of the anguish. Perhaps if I had stayed and talked to him he wouldn't have committed suicide. If I had comforted him, tried to rationalize his sense of uselessness and given him some hope of some kind, although who knows what, it might have saved him. How would I ever know? I wept. How he must have been suffering and all I could think of was Nigel.

In his note he had written the same kind of things he has talked about last night. Sarah let me read it before the police took it away. The contents were mostly to do with Coward. How much he had admired Coward. He knew that even if he had lived to be a hundred he would never achieve anything like what Coward had achieved. He knew he was not talented, the frustration of knowing this and the thought that he would live with it for the rest of his life became unbearable. He wanted fame so much, he wanted the opening nights, the friends, the adulation which he would never have then he realized he would always live with this misery. He wanted to stop his anguish and the thought of following in Coward's footsteps around his house, his hilltop spot where Coward had so easily dashed off a few classic songs and plays, just tipped him over the edge. He no longer wanted to live. If he couldn't achieve what he most wanted he didn't want to live anymore.

Obviously everyone was shocked and upset. After the body had been removed we all met in the lounge downstairs and commiserated with each other. I couldn't stop weeping in front of everybody, so I went out to the kitchen to try to recover myself, and help make tea as well as make some sandwiches.

Sarah was wonderful, she had the job of dealing with it all. The Police, the authorities, handing over his passport and his possessions, then trying to decide what they would do with regard to the funeral. The police tried to reach relatives back in London, but there didn't seem to be anyone they could contact.

Nigel arrived when we were all in the living room. We smiled warmly at each other, but he had come to help Sarah and talk to the police as well, so we had no time alone. I hadn't had a chance to ask Sarah more about him and certainly this wasn't the time. He was a great help with arranging the details and the funeral.

We hardly spoke, in front of the others, and I knew we would only be able to see each other after the horrible business was over.

Even to phone me at the house would have looked strange and I wanted to be on my own with my guilt.

I decided not to tell the others about my talk with Brian the night before or how guilty I felt about leaving him. There was really nothing they could say. Less said soonest mended, was what my mother always used to say. I spent the day going for a very long walk on my own and swimming in the ocean till I was physically exhausted. Certainly we didn't talk much at dinner that night.

They buried him in a small local churchyard the next day and as the rector had once known Noël Coward, he was told what happened. This being the tropics and in a small resort, they wanted as little fuss and attention as possible, even though there would probably be an enquiry afterwards. We all went to the service and the burial, then afterwards came back to the hotel. Our small group had been the only people there. I thought that he would have been pleased to be buried in that churchyard, not very far from Firefly. I was a basket case, I couldn't think straight and tried to stop myself from weeping every few minutes. I hadn't spoken to Nigel at all. We were both aware that I had left Brian that night to meet him so he knew what I was feeling.

However, he came over to the house for drinks with the Rector and his wife, after the burial and we had a chance to talk for a few minutes. He could see how terribly upset I was, and took my hand and squeezed it, when the others weren't looking.

"Don't feel bad Nicole, it wasn't you fault, you know" which almost set me off again.

"I know, but I could have done more to help him." I murmured.

"That's what you think now, but he must have been on the edge for a long time, because he wouldn't had all those sleeping pills otherwise."

We stood there, while the others went out on to the verandah.

He wanted to talk, to tell me more about himself. Maybe it was to distract me, but also I think he wanted me to know more about him.

His wife had died of cancer two years ago. They had come out to Jamaica after he had retired from a London corporation ten years ago, and now he had the house up for sale.

"It may take some time, because the island has now got the reputation of being dangerous, so many people are not buying because of the bad publicity. However it is now almost under control, so we will see what happens".

I turned away as I didn't want him to look at me. It was all too much. Now he had had to go through another burial. Evidently his wife had been ill for a long time and when she died, the whole village came to the funeral as they were so well-known in that area, having had local nurses in the house. She had been buried in the same churchyard.

Composing myself, I looked back at him, from the look in his eyes, I realized that maybe there may be some future for us. Like me, I sensed he was not ready for any kind of relationship. It was still too soon. But definitely the chemistry was right between us. We both felt it. I told him about Peter's death, because he had told me of his loss, so he knew exactly how I was feeling.

"Please call me if you do get back to London. It would be lovely to see you again." I said.

Well, I couldn't be more plain than that, could I?

Then he said, "Why don't I show you something of the island? You will get bored sitting around the pool all day, especially after what has happened. Perhaps the others would like to come too?"

"How kind of you. That really would be lovely." We needed his company.

So, for the remainder of our stay he took us out. Picnics to the waterfalls, through villages and towns to various beauty spots. I found out he had retired from a large corporation years ago just before Lloyds went under, thank goodness.

I was too shocked by the events, so I didn't want to sleep with him again I felt too guilty. I felt numb with the pain.

All of us felt affected by the events and tried not to discuss it too much. Whereas the others hadn't known Brian at all, and I hadn't seen him for ten years, it was the thought that we had all been with him at dinner that night. But why we hadn't noticed how upset he must have been, how moved he was, all of us talking about Coward, playwrighting and fame?

The whole group at the table had been cheerful, telling jokes, teasing each other. We had accepted the fact that Coward was a genius and that we were not and would never be, but he hadn't accepted this fact and could not accept it. I wondered what Coward would have said about his despair.

It was something everybody must have felt at one point in their lives. Often perhaps after hearing some brilliant music, or a concert pianist, a singer, a mathematician, someone whose genius you recognize immediately and leaves you stunned. However, it must be doubly hard for an ambitious pianist hearing Rubenstein, harder than perhaps for a regular patron at the concert, or an actor watching Olivier or Gielgud, and so it was for Brian. First a struggling actor and failed playwright, then becoming a travel writer. It reminded me of the short story by Somerset Maugham about a young man who after being auditioned by a prominent professional musician was told that he didn't have the talent to become a great concert pianist-which was his heart's desire. He went out and shot himself, because he didn't want to live if he couldn't fulfil his dream.

I wondered if Brian had ever read that story. I knew this place must have accelerated his depression, his feeling of failure, it was so exotic. It was an almost overpowering combination of a creative yet primitive existence coupled with fame, success, wit, money and laughter.

He had mistaken his own ambition and goals by trying to follow in Coward's footsteps. But that world would never have been opened to him unless lady luck had somehow given him a job perhaps working for Coward … as had happened to Cole Lesley who once described how luck had landed him the job of Coward's secretary.

Joan asked me about Brian one morning when we were sitting around the pool alone, a day or so after the funeral. By then I felt I could talk about what had happened.

"Did you know Brian very well, when you were working in the same company? "I know it was a long time ago but you probably remember."

"Yes I did and of course, we talked the night he arrived here."

"What did he talk about?"

"It was mostly about his career and what work he had been doing since we last met." "And? Did he appear suicidal to you?"

"No, not really. He seemed to be looking forward to seeing Firefly."

"What was his background, as far you know?"

"He got in with the wrong crowd. He knew he wasn't getting the recognition he deserved, so in desperation he used to go to certain Clubs in London and they finally threw him out because he networked like crazy but he didn't spend any money."

"Yes, I know the Clubs you are talking about, especially the Gazebo Club. It's full of poseurs and phonies. John has taken me there several times."

"He told me he used to go home and watch the video of the life of Coward until he knew it backwards. He said it was his comfort video, he'd switch it on every time he was down, which was a lot! It cheered him immensely particularly if he'd just received a rejection letter with regard to his play. All the agents rejected it politely. He was devastated. He knew if he got the right leading lady that it would be a hit."

"Then because he was so low, he began neglecting himself, he said. He neglected to polish his shoes, get his hair cut, get his clothes cleaned, to contact his family, to take any interest in anything outside the theatre. It became an obsession. He would go and see a Coward play five or six times, if he thought it was well done."

"Did you ever meet his parents, when you were working with him?"

"No, they were always out front but never came round afterwards. I think they were very snobbish. He said they had sent him to a private school which wasn't a very good one and he received training for lower level jobs in the Government and such, but he used to skip school to go theatre matinees. Finally he got a job in a box office at a provincial theatre. Then he got his first "walk-on" part in the Rep Company and he became an 'actor'. An actor, with an Equity card and Health card, he was delighted. That's when I met him. He used to go to London on his days off, to see all his fellow actors at unions meetings, to keep up his profile. It was all so futile. He couldn't afford to go to the places that Coward could afford. Then he'd read about Coward being at the Savoy that day, or with Winston Churchill or the Queen Mum and be annoyed that he hadn't heard about it. He would pour out all his frustrations to me when we were waiting backstage for our entrances and sitting in the dressing room."

"He does sound as if he was obsessed."

"But so many of us are. Even Coward was, when he was much younger. He was obsessed with Charles Hawtrey, who gave him one of his first jobs, till Charles told him to get lost. There are others also. I know someone who at 90 years of age, is still obsessed with George Bernard Shaw. He is an authority on him. He can tell you dates of plays, all the characters, all the facts about GBS anything you would want to know. He has it all at his finger tips."

"Amazing!. So what's the matter with us?"Joan laughed."I guess I was obsessed with Laurence Olivier and Vivien Leigh when I was a drama student.I can still watch her in 'Gone with the Wind" but you really have had to see Olivier, live, onstage, don't you think? His animal magnetism was electric. Unbelievable. I think he stimulated more people to become actors in my day, than anybody else, or at least to try to become actors."

Charlotte appeared with iced coffee and some delicious home baked cookies that were still warm.

"I helped the cook make these." she said, offering the plate of cookies to us. We shredded a real cocoanut to stir in with the mix."

"Oh dear, more calories" I sighed.

"They're really yummy. Anyway I'm off to the beach if you don't mind.

I prefer the beach and jumping the waves, if you don't mind" Charlotte smiled as she picked up a towel to take with her.

"All that hard work in the kitchen cooking and scrubbing is enough for today." She laughed. "And I'll have you know that I now know what you are getting for dinner too!"

"Oh do tell us" asked Joan.

"No way! That's for me to know and for you to find out."

"Thanks for bringing us the goodies anyway." I said

"I'm off, I'll be back soon." She looked so slim and pretty as she ran down the path to the beach."

"She is just lovely, Joan."

"I know and I worry about her. These days there are so many horrible people about and she is so gullible, I have to stop myself from irritating her when I ask her where she is going at night and who with. But it is only natural, especially as she has some crazy friends at drama school."

As we sat there, crunching on the cookies and drinking the ice cold coffee, Joan suddenly opened up, and talked more about the decision to put Edith in the retirement home.

"Everybody will have to decide these things when they get to a certain age. Even though she had her own little flat, it was becoming impossible. We got her a cell phone, in case of emergencies and I guess, because it was a novelty, she wanted to use it. She would phone me everyday telling me that the maid, or the helper hadn't shown up and what was she to do. She was out of milk, or bread, or gin and could I please come over and help her because she couldn't fix lunch, or she didn't want to eat lunch. It was endless. It was only a matter of time before she would have a fall I knew it. Then on top of all this, John would come home. If he was out of work the tension was pretty awful. He hates inactivity but is not very good at thinking up things to keep him occupied except of course, the bottle. One day it all reached a climax and we had to decide. It had been a particularly bad day with mother, then John comes in and says he'd had a huge row with his agent because the agent had offered him a very high paying commercial and that John had refused it. It was advertising a drug to cure some men's urinary problems. It paid thousands, but he wouldn't do it.

"I don't blame him" I smiled.

"We needed the money. Who cares anyway? Anyone who would watch it and see him would just laugh anyway, then forget about it a minute later."

"No, his fellow actors would never let him live it down. He would be ribbed forever. Can you imagine they all would be holding their private parts in mock agony every time he saw them. Actors can be cruel you know. Especially if they knew how much he got in fees."

"One day recently, we went to visit one of Edith's old friends in this theatrical retirement home, and on the way back, Edith said that she really wouldn't mind living there. She knew so many old friends there, and so she would have somebody to talk to during the day, some friends who remembered all her work and some who had worked with her." She looked over at me, trying to discern if I approved.

"It made me feel so guilty about leaving her own her own so much, so I got straight on to the people and it was all quickly arranged. They were delighted to have her and when would she like to come. So it is now all arranged. When John got this latest job, I felt I could safely leave him and take this trip she really wanted to do."

"So he won't drink while you're away?"

"I hope not. It's only when a play has been running for some time and he gets bored with it, that he starts to drink. Same as other actors, as probably you well know."

"True, and John is a wonderful actor."

"Well he can be sometimes. The trouble is that he is often very funny onstage after a few drinks and the audience, not knowing, love it. However his fellow actors don't. I don't have to tell you. It's awful when he is drinking. He goes to the pub after the show for a top up and then continues to drink until he misses the last train home. He then takes a taxi which becomes very expensive. He never knows how much he tipped the driver and lots of twenty pound bills disappear this way, and we are always living on a budget."

"Has he ever gone to see anyone about it, or to AA"

"No, he absolutely refuses as he says he doesn't have a problem, but of course he does. I was so desperate that I went to see someone."

"And?"

"He tried to help but he couldn't help me with my rage. I told him about the terrible fights we had over his drinking, the rage I left, the humiliation that he wouldn't stop even though I begged him to. He preferred drinking period. To him alcohol was more important than me.

He would drink so much that he would lose great acting jobs, and here was I longing to be offered the same level of work, the great roles.

Now, at least he is on Antabuse which he hates, but he gets sick if he drinks."

"What does Charlotte think?"

"We try not to involve her. All these fights are usually late at night, or when she is out. She knows he has a problem but it is not fair to get her upset so we down play it when she is around."

"I guess that's the only way."

"But all this is incredibly boring Nicole. You know, it is a wonder though that Coward never seemed to have a drinking problem. He didn't do drugs either. Imagine sometimes he must have been out here alone, well without one of his friends or companions, just the staff and he had no communication besides the telephone, when long distance calls probably had to be booked in advance. The phone and the Post Office, and sometimes his plays were opening on Broadway or in London!"

"I suppose if you have experienced professionals taking care of everything like Binkie Beaumont did, you just let them get on with it. Besides, sometimes he couldn't go back for tax reasons."

"Right."

"When mother was a huge success in London, she often drank more than she should but nothing like John consumes. She said it was the long runs too that were the worst. Night after night, even though the audiences were different every night and you had to quickly adjust your timing to compensate, it was the repetition that was so numbingly boring."

"We've all been there."

"She said that it was the gin that kept her going some times. If you are not working, alcohol numbs the pain, and if you are working it numbs the boredom. That's why she knew all about Larry and Ralph."

"And of course, Richard Burton and others"

The sun was getting too hot. We were being cooked.

"Let's go up and have a drink before lunch" I smiled at Joan.

"Ha, you naughty girl. I'd kill for a gin and tonic."

We climbed up the steps to the main house. I felt Joan was to become a real friend and I wanted to help her by visiting Edith a lot when she is settled into her new home. Our morning was one of those times when you know you have made a new close friend, which to me is a rare thing, one you can trust and who is sympathetic and maybe in need of a good friend too.

"Boy, I'm out of condition" laughed Joan as she slowly walked up the steps.

"No, you're not. You've just been sitting down too long and we've talked too much."

The living room was cool and we helped ourselves to the self-service bar. Sarah came in with a small bucket of ice.

"Hullo you two. I've got some news for you." she said. "The police have located a sister of Brian's who lives in London."

"Really?" I was amazed.

"They have contacted her and told her of the tragedy and the police were planning to send her Brian's belongings. However as I know you are going back tomorrow I wondered if would consider taking them instead. There is not very much, so it will be a small parcel."

"Of course, I'll do it. It will be much less painful if someone delivers them, rather to receive them in the mail."

We agreed.

Our visit had been saddened by the event but we were not above seeing how dramatic the whole week had been. Almost like a play, a rather depressing one, ending with a suicide but at least now poor Brian was out of his misery. He no longer had to feel the desire to write or to be at his own opening night on Broadway or the West End or to pass witty remarks to his followers who waited outside the stage door for him. His suite at the Savoy was no longer waiting for him and neither were his fans.

Sarah had arranged to have a head stone placed in the little cemetery and on it they put his name and underneath was written 'Actor' just in case anyone from England passed by. They would know why he had been here and think kindly of him.

I phoned Nigel to say goodbye. It was as if we both knew we would never forget that night, but circumstances had interfered and we knew that it might be possible to see each other in the future at a more appropriate time.

On the final night there, Sarah took me aside in the living room and handed me a little pink circular shell, it looked rather like a pearl ... but slightly larger.

"I want you to have this Nicole, it was in a collection of shells that Coward kept in a little case. This was one of his favourites. We found them in a drawer after we bought the house, but remember him showing them to us years ago." She handed it to me and I kissed her. "Thank you so much, it means so much. How kind of you." When I got back to London I had it mounted on a little silver chain, which I wore on special occasions.

We left the hotel early in the morning. On the way back during the long flight to London, I wondered what his sister would be like. It would be interesting to find out if they had been close or not.

The flight was endless ... we were all still wondering how Edith would react when the day came for her to go into the home. Some days she didn't seem to mind the thought at all, and then she would say something like "I don't want to be with strangers. I won't go there." But we were splitting up at the airport and I knew they had their own time to deal with such decisions.

I phoned Brian's sister to tell her I had a small packet of Brian's things, his passport and watch and so on. She suggested that I go for tea one day but asked me to wait a few weeks until she had got over the shock. I wondered what reception I would receive as I had no idea how she had reacted to the news of her brother's death. I couldn't imagine.

CHAPTER 7

▼

BACK IN LONDON

Back in London I missed Nigel terribly. I must be changing I thought. Even though my career was still the most important thing in my life, I suppose it was the exotic setting, the Coward house, with such a romantic man, it was as if I had been awakened to life all over again. My hormones were working overtime, after such lovemaking. Brian's death had been a wake-up call. But I had told Nigel not to call me because I didn't want to have a long distance relationship with not much chance of a future. Now I felt sorry. I could always call him but I resisted. I had to admit I was missing Nigel so much that Ellen suggested going out on a few dates. She and her friends would arrange it all. There wasn't any work so I was restless.

"We want you to get out more, so go! But remember blind dates can be devastating. Especially if they know your work. You never know if they like you for yourself or your reputation. But please give it a try at least."

"O.K. I will."

She then ran down a short list. She had met a handsome South African at a party last week. He was a widower and just moved to London. So he wouldn't know my work, I hoped.

"He's very nice, but not my type." Ellen laughed.

She gave me his number and I said I was a friend of Ellen.

We met in the foyer of the Café Royal. One of my favourite places as the bar off the lobby is elegant and quiet. We shook hands and he ordered two glasses of white wine. South African of course. Rather rugged face with bushy eyebrows, but nice brown eyes and nice smile. We talked about his life in Cape Town but then he started in about his wife's recent death. Oh dear, oh dear, I couldn't decide whether to be a therapist and listen, or cut him off. He was so full of his story, my smile froze and I felt dumb with boredom. It was much too soon for him to date again, someone should TELL him! Ellen perhaps. I felt sorry for him, but he should have known that details of a funeral weren't much of a turn-on.

Then she produced another guy, who had been in the navy. I like naval men. We at least had dinner together. However he had a nasty habit when talking, of quickly running his tongue across his lower lip every two minutes or so which was awful. I stared at it and nick-named him "Lizard Lips".

He habit reminded me of a lizard. I made an excuse and got out of there as soon as possible.

I told Ellen to give up with her suggestions, and preferred to be with her than those types. I felt very depressed.

Then I met Gordon at a 'call-back', that is the second call after an audition when the producer usually wants you to read more of the script. I knew and admired his work and was delighted to meet him. He knew my work too and afterwards we went on for a drink nearby. We found ourselves laughing most of the time about the latest gossip and our agents various ways of irritating us. Tony always eating on the phone was my pet peeve. Not that he was fat, he never got fat, but he was always eating.

Gordon was a rugged type too, but with wrinkly lovely eyes, and strong hands with long fingers. Grey haired, but very aristocratic looking. Classy.He knew about my Oscar, my work at Stratford, Peter's death and I knew about his divorce. His wife was not dead, but she was to him.

"She always resented me working at night. She wanted me to live, what she called a normal life."

"Well she should never have married an actor!"

"She got pregnant and back in those ancient times, you did the right thing, of course. Then she adopted another child, with my grudging permission, I had to support it after all, and those kids became her whole life."

"Oh dear of her."

"Trouble is she had no other interests. She spent her whole day taking care of them, and then when she put them to bed, she was lost."

We kept laughing about other wives and husbands which drew us together.

The following week, we both got the leads in a new situation comedy for TV. It was a series about a married couple of a certain age, who have to deal with his early retirement and how they try to avoid any conflict when he is around the house all day. There were thirteen episodes and Gordon and I were having so much fun. We rehearsed and learnt our lines together, it was such a change from going to perform in a theatre each night. We had a studio audience, but the script was sweetened by some extra laughter, just in case.

We were delighted when the series was bought for distribution in the States. It was going to be part of the British sit-coms shown every weekend on PBS.

We started sleeping together shortly after the first week. He had his own flat but we decided that we both needed our own space so we could be with each other when we wanted to, often we needed a break to be by ourselves.

However we both felt the need to be hugged every so often and make love.

Remembering Brian's sister, when I knew we were booked to have a two week hiatus in filming I called her again

"Please may I come and see you?" I asked.

"Yes,of course. She invited me for tea the following day. "I live in Maida Vale." She gave me directions on how to get there.

She lived in a flat on the top floor of a rather nice house that had obviously been converted into a flat upstairs and one downstairs.

I rang the bell.

The door was answered by a rather small woman, almost grey hair, nicely dressed in a floral cotton dress and cardigan and low-heeled shoes in beige. I just couldn't tell her age, around fifty I guessed, and I had no idea if she was older or younger than Brian.

"Hullo, I'm Beryl. Won't you come in?"

I followed her down a small hall into a sparsely furnished living room. A tabby cat got up and looked at me, then when I sat down came over and sniffed.

I put the package down on a side table by the door, rather than hand it to her.

"I brought this from the hotel. I believe the police told you what items they were sending."

"Yes, they did. Thank you for bringing it to me. You are very kind."

She ignored the package and went to the window to pull the curtain back slightly. I was pleased that the package was almost out of sight, sitting where it was, away from the coffee table and chairs facing the small gas fireplace. Obviously she wasn't going to open it while I was there, which was a relief. Still it was better that I had brought it I think, than to have it delivered in the post.

"Would you like a cup of tea?" she asked.

"That would be lovely. Thank you."

When she went into the small kitchen I had time to look around. There was a photo of Brian on a dresser and another one, both of them smiling, obviously taken years ago on the window sill. She had a rather large television set I thought, considering the size of the room. That had been a luxury buy, I bet, and a very nice polished TV stand beside it. The coffee table was glass and had several books about birds stacked on it.

She must be a bird watcher I thought.

The clock on the wall was a cuckoo clock ... from Switzerland I presumed. Probably a gift from Brian. It is sure to go off while I'm here, I thought,and made a mental note. I knew the surprise might make me laugh considering the tension, and the seriousness of the conversation we were about to have. Laughter would be deadly, even if it was only over the sudden surprise of a striking cuckoo clock. It's a wonder the cat hadn't tried to attack it, I thought.

As she came into the room with a tray, I could see she had bought some of my favourite biscuits and there was a small vanilla sponge cake as well.

A rather nice, if very conservative woman. One who makes up the backbone of England.

We talked of general matters, the weather, how long she had lived here, her cat, who was now sitting on my lap watching me eat a piece of cake.

When I told her that I had worked with Brian over ten years ago in a Rep company she was astonished. She remembered those plays ... in fact she came to see some of them. She said she remembered me but I doubt if she did because it was so long ago and the roles were quite forgettable.

It was really very difficult to start to talk about Brian.

"I always thought he was a depressive kind of person," she said.

"Mind you we hadn't been in touch for some time. He seemed to be travelling a great deal and we had a big row several years ago, which was devastating to me. We hardly spoke after that."

She smoothed down her skirt, brushing off some cake crumbs.

"Do have some more tea," she said.

Over a second cup of tea, and more biscuits, she finally told me about the break-up they had had. Evidently after their parents died, Brian started spending most of his share of their inheritance. It was their parent's life savings, and pro- ceeds from their house. She got up and went for more hot water in the kitchen. Then coming back into the room, she said

"My parents would have turned over in the grave. They were very thrifty and saved all their lives, my father even kept string and foil wrap, a habit left over from the war years. They watched their budget every day, never spending it on any kind of luxury. They always bought the cheapest brands in the supermarket, they never let their library books get overdue, and only went to the cinema about three times a year. My mother used to shop for her clothes in charity shops. So after they died, when Brian started ordering custom made shirts and suits, and dining out at expensive restaurants, I was appalled. He invited me out once and the dinner cost well over 100 pounds, I couldn't believe it. I had always saved too, because I thought he might need it. Being an actor, you never know what your income is going to be, so I thought I should be the responsible one. Now that he is gone, well that worry is at least off my shoulders." She pushed back a strand of hair behind her ear, and picked up the teapot.

"More tea?" She seemed relieved that she had got so much off her chest.

"No thank you. I've had two cups already. It was lovely tea."

I told her of our meeting and how we had talked over dinner the night before he died. How much he seemed to be enjoying Blue Harbour.

The police had told her that it had been suicide and I wondered what she thought about that. I quickly learnt.

"Actually I am surprised he didn't do it years ago." She said.

"Really? I was rather shocked.

"He was always so upset with his career. Once he told me that he was giving up the theatre, which he did of course, because it was so frustrating and he wasn't getting the parts he wanted. Then I didn't see him after we had the row, even though I tried to keep in touch with him. He just didn't want to see me. I had been too critical, I guess."

I was aware that she was sizing me up and down wondering if I knew more than she did about Brian. I reassured her.

"I hadn't seen him for ten years until he showed up in Jamaica. He didn't look well. I wondered if he had health problems."

"Well if he did, I didn't know about them and of course, now we will never know."

The cat was now purring in my lap and kneading my thigh. I lifted his paw gently to stop him, and he looked up at me curiously.

"I know we didn't get on at all over the last few years, but he was my brother after all, and really the only family member left. He owned his own flat, which I will sell as the price has tripled, so now I will have some money to spend at last."

She suddenly started to cry. It was very sad. After a minute or two she controlled herself and then came a very surprising little speech.

"You see I always envied Brian. Of course I envied his life. His travels, especially. He visited glamorous places, the Bahamas, the south of France, Switzerland, he enjoyed his life. I have had to work all my life and for once I would like to go to these places myself, before it is too late."

She had stopped crying and poured herself more tea. Her third cup.

"I have always wanted to travel but could never really afford it". She looked at me with such sad eyes and it looked as if she was going to cry again.

"I felt that as long as Brian was an actor that I should keep what savings I had just in case I might need to help him out and for any other kind of emergency. It was ironic but after my parents died we were quite rich, as their house sold for a huge price. They never had that much money in all their lives. Now I want to spend some of the money.

I tried to understand how she could have lived all these years seemingly without any kind of pleasure. She was unmarried, living a very dull existence. I did feel sorry for her. I wondered what plans she had for the evening. Nothing I suppose, just another night in front of the telly. God, how boring.

"Thank you for the tea." I really felt badly just leaving her, knowing she would open the package of Brian's belongings after I left.

"Would you like me to stay while you open Brian's things,it must be very sad for you." There I'd said it.

"No, that's alright.I know what there is. I gave him his watch years ago for one of his birthdays, and the rest I've seen. Passport etc … nothing really."

It was very hard to read her. But I had to believe her, that she was not so terribly upset, that it was no big deal.

"Would you like to open them now, and then we could go down and have a drink somewhere, a kind of a wake, if you like."

No, I thought, that's not what she wants.

Suddenly she said that she had found a playscript when she was going through Brian's belongings at his flat, the week before. "I read it in one sitting" she said. "I think it is really rather good … would you read it when you have the time?" It's called 'Waiting for Coward'.Of all the plays he wrote, I think this one is the best. He must have written it more recently. Will you read it?"

"Of course! Where is it?"

She went into the bedroom and came out with a rather battered folder.

"Here it is … there is only one copy, so perhaps I should make a copy?"

"No, no need. I can read it in a day or so and give it back."

I took it home with me and read it that evening. When I finished it I put it down, realizing that he had written an extremely good play. I was astounded. It was funny, interesting and deeply moving. I looked for a date on the script but there was none. The play was about lost years and lost opportunites. He had taken the characters from Coward's play "Private Lives" renaming them, and set the play 30 years later, when they all met accidentally in New York. The lives of each couple had changed and Brian had captured the "what might have been" feeling, of opportunities wasted and love grown old.

I made a copy of the play and gave it back to Beryl. An idea was forming in my head. If I could help Beryl get Brian's play produced at least it would be a tribute to him as ease my guilt. Over the next few days I e mailed and phoned all the people I knew who could possibly help. I called Beryl too and told her the news. She was overwhelmed and said that she wanted to help in any way she could. She was willing to help produce it, to finance the publicity and said it would be the most marvelous thing in the world if we could do it.

I took up the challenge and we agreed to work together on the project. We would meet the following week to exchange ideas and plan the future.

Both of us were determined that Brian would not have died in vain.

CHAPTER 8

▼

When I met her in town for lunch I was astonished at her appearance. She had been to a rather good hairdresser and had her hair cut short-maybe at Vidal Sassoon. She had make up on, a very good pant suit and Valentino sun glasses. I smiled when I sat down.

"What are you grinning at?" she asked.

"At your transformation! You look terrific."

"Thank you. It cost a fortune. But at least I can afford it. I feel as if Brian has given me a new lease on life. If I can't do what I want to do now, at this time of my life, when can I?"

We ordered salads and white wine. She looked around her at the other customers, I noticed she was studying how other women were dressed.

"You know, for years I didn't care what I looked like really … I didn't have any good clothes and I, just didn't care. But maybe Brian has taught me a thing or two … I want to look well dressed and sophisticated-especially if I have to talk to producers. What do you think?" She turned to me for approval.

"Definitely. It is the only thing to do."

The following weeks were exhausting. We found ways to get to see producers and when Beryl mentioned she had the money for a co-production, at last one producer said he would take it on. I was amazed at Beryl's talent to negotiate and focus on specific details. She persisted, no matter how many rejections she got. It was as if this had been part of her nature laying dormant in her psyche somewhere, suddenly she developed a knack for pinning people down, asking for confirmation on paper, making dates, booking people to see. Not aggressively, but firmly. Everything happened as she had planned it and I only felt thankful that I might have helped her start living her real life at last. She had a project which she believed in whole heartedly, and that made all the difference. Her drive, her persistence, her doggedness reminded me of that mother in the novel who finally got her daughter's manuscript published, posthumously. It really did look like she was finally going to get Brian's play produced.

The effort was fraught with broken promises and false hopes. One producer said he'd do it, and the next week he changed his mind. The director who was so keen to do it, went off on tour for six months. The theatre we wanted was no longer available. People who said they would get back to us, never did, and we were astonished at the genuine lack of reliability in trying to confirm things. But we were both determined to get the play on no matter what. I wondered if we had gone crazy. It took us another four weeks but finally we found what we wanted. A producer!

Gordon and I were just finishing up the television series, which we hoped would be renewed next season, however he was offered a lead role in a feature film, with money he couldn't refuse, so he left shortly afterwards to do the movie in Spain. That's show business! I was on my own again, but this time I had found a real project that had to be completed. It suddenly came to me about loss, especially of a loved one, the trick is to surround yourself with so many close friends who can offer so much support, it gives you a cushion and they give you a different kind of love.

CHAPTER 9

▼

"Why Must the Show go on?"

—Coward

Ellen was away for several weeks on tour again. She always called as soon as she got back to London. So as usual, we met for lunch.

She looked well even though she had put on some weight. Her black turtle neck sweater and black pants, together with a large topaz on a gold chain around her neck, looked very chic, against her red hair which was glossy and well cut.

"I have an announcement to make. A very important one, Nicole."

I turned to her, waiting for the dramatic words she was about to announce.

"I have decided to leave the theatre for good. This time I mean it. This time it is final."

"Oh?" I was speechless.

"Maybe those magic moments in the theatre were great, but I have found a replacement for my passion. Maybe I'm a silly old woman who doesn't know what she's doing. [she hadn't reached 50] I don't want this shitty life any longer. It is all shitty self sacrifice. I know what I know, which isn't much it seems."

Then she told me about Ian. "I am really in love this time Nicole … this is it. He is a handsome bloke and very wealthy. He owns three hotels, a yacht, an art gallery and he thinks I am wonderful. I have been trying to think of the word for how I am feeling."

"Oh yes", I smiled, she was feeling no pain.

"It's Joy! Joy! What a wonderful word. So simple. I am in love! What more do we need, but how difficult to find it. This wonderful man absolutely feels right. He fulfils my every need. He wants me, he entertains me, he makes me feel special and who does that for you in the theatre? When I wake up in the morning, I look forward to the day now rather than want to bury my head under the pillows. Will you come to the wedding?"

I was astonished. "Wedding? When?"

"Next month. We are getting married in Venice. You must come."

"Venice?"

"Yes, he wants it there."

"Now wait a minute", I put down my glass. "Why haven't you told me about him? We are best friends, remember and you haven't bothered to tell me anything!"

"I didn't want you to talk me out of it, that's why. I can hear you. "Take it slowly, be careful." I know. Just like the last time.

"I still think we could have discussed it"

"I was on tour, remember?"

"Then how did you meet him?"

"He was staying at the Randolph Hotel in Oxford, when we were there. A few of us used to go there for a drink after the show … he was sitting at the bar one night, and we got into conversation. From then on we used to meet there every night until he had to leave."

"Where does he live?"

"Would you believe it? In Italy!"

"An Italian?" I gasped, thinking of my affair with Carlo …

"No, don't worry. He's a Canadian, but he hates Canada. So he lives in Italy."

"What does he do?"

"Darling, he is so rich, he doesn't have to do anything!"

"But he must do something … to stay alive." I looked at her and she was looking radiant. I felt so pleased for her, but very concerned. I started to look around the room to see if anyone was listening … we were the only two left."

"I'm amazed you haven't told me before!" I shook my head. I was trying to see into the future and determine if I would have to pick up the pieces before she headed back to search for theatre work again.

"Are you really sure?" I tried not to be a Cassandra.

"Absolutely. I know it is the right thing. I suddenly realized that after a certain age, working in the theatre is all very well if you are a star, a celebrity, earning a living, being recognized for your talent and work in a normal kind of way, but who will remember you? Your brilliant interpretation. Even … if you play Cleopatra as well as Peggy Ashcroft, your work will still forgotten in a few years. Look at Vivien Leigh … all her work is forgotten except for her work in 'Gone with the Wind'.

Look at all the wonderful Shakespearean actresses of the past. Does anyone remember Dame Sybil Thorndike anymore? Or Helen Hayes, Ethel Barrymore?"

"But surely that's not the point. You act, because you have to act. You shouldn't care whether you are remembered or not … it is in the act of doing it that matters."

"Most actors don't seek immortality, they just know that they want to act."

"But, after a certain age, you can't expect the big roles anymore, even if you could play them. It's this whole business of rejection too. After years and years of it you wonder why you put up with it. You know I still have to audition. That really put the cap on it for me. I am not going on auditions anymore. It's finished. You have to be born into a theatrical family to have a head start of some kind. Someone who can pull a few strings for you. How many strings do I have to pull? I'm still touring for heaven's sake."

She was speaking the truth.

"After a lifetime in the theatre what do you have to show for it?"

"You never know. You probably created a character that some child will remember all their lives. Your definitive performance of a role … that people will carry to their graves. I will remember Richard Burton's "Hamlet" for the rest of my days as the definitive one."

"That's because you never saw John Gielgud." She went on … "It is so humiliating. Also your memory starts to go at about my age."

"Don't be ridiculous."

"Well, it does. What can be more humiliating than to forget your lines in front of a thousand people out front, and your fellow actors looking at you onstage?" Nothing. Its like coming second in a Marathon. People feel sorry for you and the whole world is watching." Then there is the bitchiness, how some of those actresses can turn on you so totally. It can affect you physically. It is so totally physical. That's why actors laugh and joke a lot amongst themselves. It is the tension of juggling your work with your memory, juggling the passion you have with your aging body."

"You aren't even 50!" I joked.

"I don't care. I can't take it anymore. Fame is not on my agenda. I may become a famous hostess. Who knows, I could become the Italian version of Elsa Maxwell? I'll give marvellous parties and eat myself silly."

She put more lipstick on and looked at her hair in the mirror.

"I want to meet this man", I demanded. "When can I meet him?"

"Tomorrow night. He is coming into London tomorrow night."

"Great. The sooner the better" I was very curious.

"Yes, let's all go out for dinner."

"Sounds good. If he agrees to it."

"He will. I've told him all about you. He wants to meet you. He was watching that night when you won the Academy Award. Way back then." She winked.

I ignored it. She put her hand out to touch my arm. Then followed in a rush …

"But please, don't put him off … Be nice to him … Aren't you happy for me?"

"Yes, of course … it's not just the sex is it Ellen?"

"Pulease Nicole. What do you take me for? Of course not … he is so full of life. He is theatre himself. He is full if initiative, ideas, energy, ambition, it is just so stimulating to be with him. Time passes in a flash. I don't remember time anymore and you know how I always used to count the minutes every day waiting for that bloody phone to ring."

"What do you like most about him?" I was curious.

He is just so bright, He is kind and considerate, he understands what you tell him immediately. He is quick, in other words. I am really just over the moon. He likes me, he didn't say he loved me after the first ten minutes either."

"How old?" I was suddenly suspicious.

"He says he is 55, but maybe he could be 60. But his maturity is his charm. He knows the world. It is obvious that he has been around."

"Not married, I hope?"

"Divorced. Ten years ago."

"Who could have given such a man up? There must be something wrong somewhere."

"Oh, really Nicole! Don't be like that. She left him for a tennis pro."

"No! You're joking!"

"Honestly … I'm not kidding. They were living in Toronto, she was bored and she ran off with a young tennis pro to Florida. Imagine."

"I can't!"

"She must have been mad!"

"She is probably regretting it now!" She laughed.

"No children?"

"No, thank goodness. However he is not opposed to the idea. He says living in Italy makes him see how important children are to the Italians. They adore them and he is caught up with the whole thing."

I was really quite shocked to hear all this. It is so different from the Ellen who was so ambitious and determined on a stage career. It was as if she had become another person. A different Ellen, maybe an older and wiser Ellen. It must be love. She never, ever wanted to have children. Wouldn't even discuss it.

It was then that I had to tell her about Brian. I hadn't wanted to break any bad news while she was so full of her good news, and happiness.

"Oh, how sad." She looked at me with troubled eyes. "It's almost unbelievable that he would be so depressed. We got along very well, he always kept to himself though, not much of a talker. He excused himself on the grounds of his fear of forming new friendships, which he gallantly described as his fear of being made unhappy. I think some woman must have made him suffer, so he thought all the rest were like her."

I told her how he had said he could never become famous because he knew he didn't have the talent.

"That doesn't mean anything these days. He must have known that, if you get a great P.R. campaign and use those wizards at advertising agencies. It doesn't matter anymore if you can act or not." She wiped her mouth, then continued.

"You see how awful this profession has become?" Well that's why I've had enough."

I told her about contacting Beryl, as well as the news that Brian had written a play.

"I'd be curious to meet her", she said, "but I doubt if anything can be done about his play, do you?"

"Well, I will try to help her as much as I can."

"Just more heartbreak probably. What a business. It is a crazy world filled with all these unrealistic theatre types. Producers, actors, playwrights, still struggling. Then perhaps, they have one big success, they feel they've hit the big time, then nothing again for months, if ever.

"Ian is the sanest person I have ever met, besides being rich." She tried to make a joke of it. "It is the constant rejection, the failure to get that role that you really want and are the most suitable for, the disappointments, the long runs when you are bored out of your mind, it all adds up to zero. Sorry, I'm being repetitive. Let's get out of here." She stood up.

We gathered up our things, paid the bill and staggered out. Later that night, as I lay in bed, I thought over what she had said. Yes, she was right in a way. Who cares if your interpretation of Lady Macbeth is the best in ten years, or your Cleopatra, whether you get good notices, or if you are going to be cast in next year's season? It is such a wretched business unless you are a star. A star, who can pick and choose what role they would like to do next. Agents turning down contracts for you!

The trouble is that the fleeting wonderful moments onstage just do not match the misery of weeks of waiting for work, and living a rather drab, expectant life, watching the economic future, as well, until suddenly you are too old to do anything else, and nobody wants you anymore. Maybe she is much wiser than I thought. Somerset Maugham once told a young actress who asked him for some advice about her career and how she could get work.

"Marry a rich American and move to the States!" was his answer.

CHAPTER 10

───────── ▼ ─────────

Beryl and I went to see the producer next day who was producing Brian's play. He told us he had got the cast we wanted, and we were overjoyed. Brian wouldn't have believed it. He had written down in the script the names he wanted against every character, so that made much easier. Just maybe the gods were with us.

When I got home there was the usual message from Gordon checking up to see if I was O.K. but still no message from Ellen as to whether we were going for dinner or not. Perhaps she was still waiting to hear from Ian. I was looking forward to meeting him I wondered if he would be anything like Nigel.

I kept thinking that I was a fool not to have kept in touch with him. He must be very popular and have many friends, yet the chemistry between us was something special, we both knew it but then I was the one who went away and told him not to call.

But I was pleased for Ellen. I knew exactly how she felt. When she went on about Ian I couldn't help thinking that what she said made sense. I tried her number again but she had forgotten to turn on her answerphone which was unusual. However if she was giving up the theatre then she wouldn't be interested in any more messages.

How ironic if she was offered a great part, I thought.

I stacked up the dishwasher then went into the bedroom to try to tidy up my closet. I never could hang all my skirts together, on separate hangers, or my blouses ... I just didn't seem to have the time. So now I would. I tried putting all my slacks together, until I went to try and find a favourite pair then they would all get mixed up again. I wonder how other woman manage. A maid would help of course. I imagine Ellen will have a maid if Ian is that rich. How really wonderful to have a maid to keep your closets in order. What a dream to have a place tidy and clean when you come home. I began to feel sorry for myself. I could afford to have a maid to put my clothes away and clean the house, but I really didn't want someone else here in the place, someone else handling my clothes, so I didn't. So what was wrong with me? Yes, I was also very dissatisfied with my life, then hearing Ellen's romantic future and escape from London had made me slightly envious.

A wedding, happiness, a new life. I wondered should I try for it too.

The phone rang at last. It was all set. We were to meet at Rules at 7.p.m. Ellen had already made a reservation. Rules, my favourite. She must have known it. It was Graham Green's favourite too, he always celebrated his birthday there when he was in London. I wondered if the fascination with the place would ever diminish. The décor, the ambience were exceptional, as long as we weren't seated beside some loud tourists who were in cut off jeans, with cell phones which they might use while eating. It drove me crazy, their conversations! just to tell someone where they were, what they were doing,(eating) what they were drinking(usually their own bottle of water)and where they were going next.

I started to dress. What to wear? The black of course. Hair up or down? It had grown a bit so I could put it up now. I swirled it up and clipped it with a diamond stage clip. I felt that this was going to be a rather stressful evening so I hoped I wouldn't say anything I'd regret. Once the words are out, you can never retrieve them. Ellen would never forgive me.

Pushing open the door into Rules is a pleasant experience ... you walk into a lovely atmosphere that never fails to charm. The fireplace is the first thing you see, often lit in winter, the gleam from the polished brass fender and various brass surrounding it make it seem like something out of the past century. The pretty bar with huge bowl of fresh flowers, the paintings, the statues, the smooth polish of the staff, makes into an occasion. I immediately felt better.

There they were sitting in the first booth. Ellen had on a cream pantsuit, a pearl choker, pale pink lipstick with her hair all fluffed up after a shampoo, she looked wonderful. Ian stood up as I approached with some difficulty as he was hemmed in by the table.

"How do you do?" I offered him my hand. I remember reading somewhere that you can always tell a gentleman because he waits to see if you offer your hand. I wondered if it was still considered bad form for a man to offer his hand first.

He waited. "How do you do? Come and sit down. We have Ellen's favourite table." I sat down and looked at them both. They made a handsome couple. He was handsome, very tanned and greying at the temples but very well-dressed and healthy looking. I felt slightly embarrassed as if I shouldn't have been there with them.

"We thought you'd like to come here as Ellen has said how much you both like the place."

"Rather! The best!" I smiled and liked him a lot.

After the waiter had taken our orders, we started talking first about what was playing in the theatres and then what we both thought about what was playing in the theatres. Ellen was the first to say that there was no play which she would want to be in, even if she had been asked.

"What's happened to the West End is rather like what's happened on Broadway. The plays are for the tourists and they come in droves to see musicals and revivals. The serious stuff is at the National or the Royal Court. The golden age of the West End is over. We will never see that scene again", said Ellen.

"The time we read about when Olivier, Richardson and Sybil Thorndike were playing in Shaw's plays or Ibsen or Galsworthy are gone. It was a magical time and it is just one of those things that is in the past now."

I tried to change the subject a little and ask about Ian and his career. I didn't want to appear too curious as I knew I would learn it all from Ellen and he might think I was too nosey ... but he didn't seem to mind.

He had made his fortune in real estate in Canada, even though he knew what great things were was happening up there, he was more interested in travelling and finding new places to live.

"How long have you lived in Italy", I asked, hoping he didn't think I was cross-questioning him.

"Two years."

"Do you speak Italian?"

"A little. But everyone speaks English these days. There's no problem really."

He gave the impression of being very well-travelled and rather resigned to obvious questions such as mine. Our dinners arrived and we watched with glee as he tried to remove the paper crown from the lamb chops.

"I love this place!" as I dived into my steak and kidney pie, which was also surrounded by a white pleated paper crown.

"Oh, I forgot to order fried onions!" laughed Ellen.

"Why fried onions?" asked Ian.

"Because in Graham Greene's novel, 'The End of the Affair', the couple fall in love over grilled onions in this restaurant ... It is so romantic."

"I know about the novels, but I don't remember that scene." he said.

Wow what a nice guy! He was crazy about Ellen I could tell. He kept watching her, smiling at her, laughing at her jokes. Many of which I had heard before.

We had another bottle of wine then went on to discuss their wedding.

I tried not to comment when they were setting the date … like 'Oh no, that's much too early', or 'No, you can't do that.'

"I think you could invite more people, they may not come but they would be hurt to be left out. Anyway everyone likes an excuse to go to Venice."

"I wonder who will come actually", said Ellen. "Most of my friends are out on tour or too poor to come if they are not."

It was almost bizarre in the fact that I knew Ellen so well, we had been through all the same things together for so long, that this was something completely different.

A new life, a complete change. Venice. A life in Italy. New horizons with a new man. It was rather a shock.

The waiter came with the bill and we two went up to the washroom. We were giggling as we knew it would be horrendously expensive. We used to come to Rules, years ago when we were broke, then we would just order appetizers for the main course, pretending we were on a diet. Now the prices had nearly doubled but it was still worth it.

Rules always lit the 'fire in my belly'. It filled me with stimulating enthusiasm as if the spirits in the place were all still there. I had an overwhelming urge to keep on persisting in the theatre. I couldn't tell Ellen as she was about to give it all up. Walking down the stairs I felt it again.

Next day I met Ellen alone to talk of planning the event … Where would they have the wedding?

"I know just the place. On the rooftop at the Danieli."

"Oh yes please. Overlooking the water."

"Well it would be hard not to overlook the water in Venice", I remarked.

Next day we went shopping as I wanted to buy her a present. We were walking along Piccadilly after tea at Fortnum and Masons. The twilight was fading and the street lamps were coming on. It looked like rain.

Suddenly I saw it. It was Michael's red sports car I automatically read number plates of every red Mercedes sports car, My heart leapt into my throat and I could feel the blood leave my face. I stopped and watched it speed along the street, passing through the traffic lights by the Royal Academy.

What's wrong? said Ellen, turning around to face me.

"I just saw Michael's car!"

"Michael? You mean that jerk who dumped you so heavily ages ago?"

"Who else?"

"I thought you were well over him. He nearly destroyed you, Nicole."

"I know' But it was a shock to see his car."

"What?"

"I just saw it pass by."

"How do you know it was him?"

"The number plates."

"But he may have sold the car."

"Then there would be different number plates, wouldn't there."

"I don't know."

I felt weak. I needed to sit down. "Let's go in here."

It was a small bar where there were some seats at the back. I ordered a scotch. Ellen remained silent. I guess she knew not to talk.

He must be back in London. After he had totally wiped me out with his cruelty. I still couldn't stop the wild beating in my chest.

"Forget it", said Ellen. "Forget you ever saw the car. That's over, finished, you have moved on, remember."

Yes, I did remember. She was right. I have moved on. There is no way it would ever happen again. The drink felt good and calmed me down. So off we went again.

The thought that he had been so close. It was as if I'd seen a ghost. It was over and he shouldn't be anywhere near central London. It wasn't his area. Someone told me he had moved to Norwich.... the further the better. Yes, Ellen was right. It was over and unless he had run me down I wouldn't have spoken to him.

But it made me nervous that he was in London.

I was still vulnerable. The day he walked out of my life was the best thing that could have happened to me. I was a free woman. No more ruled by a tyrant who could hurt me as nobody else ever could.

"Do you remember that story by Somerset Maugham ... 'Of Human Bondage'? Well, I was as bad as Philip ... the man who couldn't stop loving that terrible person?" I said to Ellen.

"Yes, I know. Betty Davis played her, and Leslie Howard played Philip. There is no point in torturing yourself just be pleased you are out of it."

"But that fever is still in me and it is petrifying."

"Forget it. Just leave it. It was just a shock that's all. Just get on with your life."

CHAPTER 11

▼

"Don't Put Your Daughter On The Stage, Mrs. Worthington"

—Coward.

Next morning, after some coffee and toast, I decided I needed a long walk. I decided to go see my agent but he was out.

As I walking down Charing Cross Road it started to rain. I crossed over and went into Foyle's Bookshop. Right inside the door, on the ground floor is the travel section. What a coincidence. I picked up a book about Venice and flipped through the pages. The photos were wonderful. I wondered how long I would stay for when I went out for the wedding. It would be lovely to see all these places and I thought it would be fabulous to go out to the beach, the Lido, as well. I remember the film Death in Venice and the scenes at the magnificent hotel on the Lido. This time I might stay there. Why not?

It was the last time I would ever see Venice perhaps. I had too many memories of when I went there with Michael.

I walked on down to Cambridge Circus where the wind whipped around the corner and turned my umbrella inside out again! I had just bought a new one! What a climate. I looked up at the building where my first agent had his offices. It was a walkup and in those days five flights of stairs were no problem. He was a greasy type with a dirty office. I can't even remember his name even though I remember where his office was. Wouldn't it be lovely to be able to tell these blokes that you had won an Academy Award and that they had absolutely nothing to do with your success. All those horrible minutes waiting in their offices being treated rudely when you were so broke and desperate. It was no surprise that Ellen was getting out of it.

"Good morning, Nicole!" I turned to see someone I didn't know. It often happened, a fan who thought because they knew you, that you would automatically know them.

"I'm sorry" I don't think we've met, have we?" I turned to walk on, but the woman stopped me with her hand on my arm ...

"Please, I mean you no harm ... I just wanted to say how much I like your work. You were marvellous in that film ... what's the name?"

I named it.

"Yes, that's the one. I just thought it was great. Please can you spare a minute? I was going to write to you but I didn't know your address, so this is really a coincidence. I go to classes at the Actor's Centre which is just around the corner from here and I often hoped I would see you there ... My name is Jane. Jane Eastern. I was a friend of Brian Bailey. Remember? He was the actor who died in Jamaica. It was in the papers that you were out there at the same time ... is that right?"

My blood froze. Who was this woman? She appeared to be about 45, rather dumpy with a shabby coat and a fake fur hat pulled down over what looked like red hair. She had pulled down her umbrella and the wind was swishing it around her legs.

'Yes, I knew Brian. It was all very sad."

"Look, please, could you spare a minute. I really want to talk to you. It is most important and I'm sorry to disturb you."

She looked a little mad, but my curiosity was piqued, so I pointed across the road to a café and said "Let's get a cup of coffee then."

We crossed the road and found a table near the door. After we got the coffee, and she had put all her belongings down on a nearby chair, she took out a piece of paper from her purse and handed it to me.

It was a letter from Brian written about a year ago. He had written to her on Garrick Club stationery ... so someone had taken him to the Garrick Club once where no doubt, he had nicked some of the paper.

I felt sorry that she must have thought he was a member being an actor and in the theatre in London. I was very surprised at the contents of the letter especially as I always thought Brian had been gay.

At least he had the pleasure of being entertained in the Garrick Club by someone who must have thought enough of him to invite him there.

The letter was a confession after all. Evidently Jane had been in love with him for years and had become a kind of groupie following him around the country, attending each theatre and seeing each play he was in.

I wondered why he hadn't told her that he was gay earlier to get rid of her but now it seemed evident that he really liked having an admiring fan, even though he was indeed gay.

"But how did this relationship develop exactly? Did you ever sleep together?" I asked quite openly. Get it over with I thought.

"Well, no we never did. He said it wasn't right to sleep together before we were married."

"What on earth had Brian being playing at?" I wondered.

"He was the sweetest man on earth and he was such a brilliant actor. I saw everything he ever did."

I didn't want to appear impatient but who was I dealing with here? A crazy?

"You must have been very upset about his death." 'An obvious remark', I groaned inwardly.

"More coffee?"

"No thanks"

I got up to get another cup. It was at least hot and the weather outside looked grim. The rain was now teeming down. Better to stay here for a bit. It was proving quite entertaining. I couldn't believe Brian in this new light. What you don't know about people. It's amazing.

She continued "Brian's auntie used to work for Noël Coward and she adored him. She was a housekeeper for him for awhile and she used to tell Brian all the stories about him and what a glamorous life he lead. All the people who phoned him … she used to answer the phone while working there…. and he was brought up to think that no one lived a more luxurious life than Coward."

"So why are you telling me all this?"

"Because you might be able to help me."

"In what way?"

She took off her fur hat and shook her hair free. I looked at her more closely. She was rather pretty, in an odd sort of way. Her hands were shaking, she was very nervous and looked like she was about to break into tears at any moment.

"Well, since he has gone, I miss him terribly. We were planning to get married and now my Mum says that I should try to find out who his lawyer was, to see if he left me any money …"

"Oh, so that's it!" I thought.

She went on ... "Mum says that if he was serious then he would have left something for me in his will. I'm sorry I know what you are thinking, but I could really do with some money, you know. I keep trying for auditions but nothing happens.

"You are in the theatre too, then are you?" I looked at her through new eyes. "If you could see her through my eyes", the song from Cabaret, shot through my brain at that moment ...

"Yes. I don't make much money, though."

The poor girl. Someone should tell her. Will she be still trying when she is 70 I wondered? Like those little old ladies who serve drinks in the theatres at intermission ... Although they are now disappearing as the theatres are modernized ... Those woman knew their theatre history though. They were like walking dictionaries. Names and shows, from Ivor Novello to Cameron Mackintosh, and who played who.

She looked at me with two sad brown eyes. It was hard not to feel sorry for her. Like a sad Labrador who wanted to be stroked and taken for a walk. I wanted to make her feel better as I realized she really had nothing much in her life. Beryl had said nothing about Brian leaving money to anyone else ... I would probably have told her to check this girl out.

"Did your mother ever meet Brian?" Surely the woman would have more sense?

"No, she never did ... She was always going to come with me but never did. The places were so far away, Manchester, Glasgow and Scotland."

Brian could never stay with me after the show, because he was committed to staying at his digs. So I would catch the last train home and Mum couldn't take the travelling at that hour."

"Has your mother tried to contact anyone about the money?"

"She phoned Equity, but they had no contact and she phoned The Stage but they didn't know either."

I didn't know what to say. It really wasn't my business but I felt sorry for her. She obviously missed Brian enormously and had no work on the horizon.

"Is your mother working?" I asked.

"Yes, she still does a bit of housekeeping ... but mainly she writes plays. She has written 6, but none of them have been produced yet."

"May I ask how old she is?"

"She's in her 70s and she does get very discouraged at times. But then I keep reminding her of Grandma Moses and how she became famous."

"She still writes plays in her 70s. What are these plays about?"

"They're mostly romantic comedies … or about the theatre. Although the last one is about euthanasia."

"Does she have an agent?"

"She is still trying to get one. It is only a matter of time."

I was deciding what to tell this woman. It was obvious that I could ask Beryl about the money but should I get involved. If I told Beryl about her and her mother she might back off immediately. But meeting someone who was in love with your brother might interest her as she probably didn't know about Jane and her passion.

Suddenly a picture flashed through my mind of the rows upon rows of back-yards of those small semi-detached houses you see from the train as you are coming into London. Tiny little houses. I always wonder what they are all doing in those tiny living rooms. Maybe all those housewives are sitting at the kitchen table, all writing plays or musicals, or both. Or of they aren't playwrights, they're aspiring novelists, writing novels. The scene boggles the mind. I find it profoundly depressing. You imagine that they must be equally depressed but maybe they are not! Maybe they are all perfectly happy, thank you very much … It reminds me of Coward's play. 'This Happy Breed', except the elegance and beauty of a young Celia Johnson seemed incongruous in such a suburban setting. I thought that perhaps Jane's mother lived in one of these houses and maybe spent her time, not watching the telly but writing her plays with the dream of having one of them done in the West End. Surely if the gods were kind she might stand a chance. I was tempted to ask Jane to let me read one of them but thought it would be too embarrassing if, indeed, they were very bad.

But for some reason I wanted to do something for her. I had been lucky, I had been at the right place at the right time. But they were still way out there, looking in and finding nothing.

"If you give me your phone number, I will try to find out something for you, if I can." I looked at her.

Her mouth turned down and she bit her lip still trying not to cry.

"Thank you so much. We would really appreciate it. It's not that we are poverty-stricken or anything like that, but even though Brian didn't mention it in his letter, he must have thought about our circumstances."

I wonder. He must have because he wrote that letter to her eventually. It must have been a difficult thing to do. How do you reject someone who really seems to love you? Especially if they are not totally crazy and this woman didn't seem to be. She would have made someone a good wife, I expect.

I got up, smiling at her while collecting my things. It had stopped raining, the streets had been washed clean. She followed me out of the café.

"Thank you for your time, Nicole. I really appreciate it."

"Not at all. It was interesting time. I call you in a few days."

We said goodbye and she ran for a bus just pulling in.

I watched her dig for her ticket. I missed the wonderful old Routemaster buses … where you could hop on the back platform just as it was leaving, saving a really boring ten minute wait for the next one … They were part of old London, now gone forever.

CHAPTER 12

▼

That evening I phoned Beryl. She was full of news. The producers were going ahead with Brian's play and she was over the moon. The rehearsals wouldn't start for another three months but the production meetings were taking place and the P.R. was shaping up.

In the meantime, she was selling her flat and moving further in to town.

"Have you had any offers yet?" I enquired.

"No, but the agent is bringing two more people over in about half-an–hour."

"Great, Beryl.... can we meet for lunch this week?" I thought it would be better to see her face to face to tell her about Brian's 'girlfriend'.

"Of course. Just name the day and place."

"Rules, of course. 1pm, Thursday."

"See you then."

It was only two days away but I had thought about how I would approach the subject. I really had no idea how she would react at the news. Anything to do with money is always a touchy subject. She may be furious I even talked to Jane at all. Well we'll see ... I'm talking to myself again these days. It is always a sign I should be working.

Then the next curious thing happened. Tony did call me again and this time it was even more difficult.

Oh dear, it was incredible how difficult it was.

I immediately phoned Ellen.

I have been offered the lead in Terence Rattigan's play 'The Deep Blue Sea'.

Ellen knew the part. "A wonderful part. I remember seeing Googie Withers do it years ago. Or am I dreaming? Was it Peggy Ashcroft? But you may not want to do it. Read it first!"

She was right. I read it through that day and it is a wonderful part but I knew I wouldn't do it. I poured myself a glass of wine and called her back that night.

"You were right … it is a wonderful part but just too close to what happened to me. I can't play her every night it would be too painful. Yes, I know it's only a play but it much too soon. I haven't got over Michael yet and I'm certainly not going to try and commit suicide. Do you think I'm mad?

"No, of course you are not. It is a powerful play, and a great part but I don't see how you can do it. You will be a nervous wreck. The lines, think of the lines … they are so close to what you went through. Even though you are a professional … it is much too close to you. It would bring it all back."

"Shit! Maybe I should at least try?"

"No, you cannot learn those lines. Go through those emotions. It would be dreadful. Listen to me … for once."

Tony was annoyed, but seemed to understand. Oh dear, why is life so complicated. You wait for a great part and it suddenly comes along but there is a huge glitch … if it isn't something personal, then there is always some kind of dilemma that has to be sorted out.

The lunch with Beryl went well. I had the usual smoked salmon with scrambled eggs, they do it so well, and Beryl had the steak and kidney pudding which I helped her finish. We finished off with most sinful dessert, sharing a summer pudding, with extra cream and raspberries.

"No, I have a copy of Brian's will and there is certainly nothing in it about this poor girl," she said after I had told her everything. "I think it is an incredible story. Are you sure she's not just making it up? I mean how would we know? There were no photographs in his flat except family ones, and there were no letters, how do we know it isn't all made up?"

"I think if you met her, you would see quickly enough that she is genuine."

"Oh, I don't think that's a good idea, do you? Although it is tempting to meet someone who was so in love with Brian. She probably knew him better than I did, and she did see more of his acting than I ever did."

"Well, I can easily arrange it if you like. I really think she would like to meet you as she thought so much of Brian, she want to talk about him of course, if that wouldn't be too upsetting."

"She is an actress, you say?"

"Used to be but didn't get very far."

"Let me think about it for a day or two. I'm sorry not to have good news for her. Poor thing. Brian really was abit stupid leading her on like that."

"I guess he felt sorry for her and also liked her coming to see him when he was acting out in the boondocks. We both know what a difference it makes to have someone out front, especially when you are playing in a theatre, miles from anywhere."

"Who else would do that? Certainly not his agent."

"I will break the news to her and see what she says about meeting you too."

"Let me get this." she reached for the bill.

'Please, I want to."

"No, next time."

That night, I called Jane and broke the news.

"Well Jane, I talked with Beryl, she said that she will get back to me in a couple of days about all this."

She was very quiet I knew she would be in floods of tears and soon as we hung up.

"As soon as she does, I will phone straight away."

"Thank you very much Nicole. I am very grateful for your help"

There was nothing more to say. I felt terrible. Maybe I can find her a job, an acting job, to cheer her up. I suddenly thought of Brian's play. There was a small walk-on part of a cleaning woman who had two or three funny lines … maybe she could read it for it.

I went to bed feeling slightly relieved that I could possibly help her. It was too late to call Beryl but I'd call tomorrow.

CHAPTER 13

▼

'The best thing about London, is Paris.'

—Dianne Vreeland.

Ellen had gone to Paris with Ian for three days, now she was back with her trousseau. I couldn't wait to see it.

"Come over for tea" I said, when she phoned. "I want to see everything."

I wanted to share in her happiness, even though I was not sure it would last. Living in Italy will have its disadvantages and she hasn't even thought about learning the language.

"What is this?" I held up a gorgeous piece of blue satin, with lace, ribbons and bows. That is the French equivalent of a teddy … not much for 200 pounds is it?"

"200 pounds, you must be crazy!"

"I don't get married every day of the week, you know! It is sooo pretty, I had to have it!"

She showed me all her purchases, they were all divine. I was slightly envious. The workmanship on the garments were so fragile and fine. Only the French could make such things.

"Now let's get down to the invitations … who have we forgotten?"

We went through the list of all her friends. Most of them I didn't know. Lots in Normandy and Tuscany. I was surprised just how many people had escaped living in Britain.

"Do you keep in touch with all these people?"

"Of course! I go to stay with them too. It is interesting to see how other people live in France. I love the place. Maybe Ian will buy a place there. He used to own a vineyard once but it didn't work out. After he bought it, they watered the wine and it was no good for export so he sold it and then they made better wine without the water."

She rattled on and on and I shared her good spirits and enthusiasm.

Suddenly I missed Peter very much. It just swept over me like a cloud. I think it was because Ellen so happy and I realized just how much Peter had made me happy. Being together was usually a pleasure and I'd forgotten the joy of being with someone who loves you.

"What's wrong?" Ellen sensed it.

"Oh nothing, just that I need some fresh air. Shall we go out for a walk? I needed to get out of the house and breathe in big drafts of fresh air. Always makes you feel better … I didn't want to dampen her spirits at this particular time with talking about Peter.

"Let's go!" and she was out the door, holding it open for me. I guess the mood had passed. I was feeling better already.

Walking along the street we started talking about theatre again. How much the acting of our previous generation had stimulated us to go into the theatre. It was those performances that made us want to emulate them. Such wonderful actors, are there any left anymore, who could inspire you like they did?

"But when you analyse it, Nicole, don't you think we were in love with the glamour of the theatre … it gave us the stimulus of the seeing these wonderful people, because we didn't have anything else in our lives. We wanted that glamour."

"It could be."

"The reason why people still love actors like Noël Coward is because he seemed to have such a glamorous life, whereas we didn't." He was a great talent, very witty and a great performer but his life was also interesting. That's why people still read about him, and others like him."

I listened to her and agreed. At least she was getting on with her life, living a role of her own not in someone else's shoes. She was carving a life out for herself. I often thought the reason I loved acting was because you do live in someone else's shoes and you may have a 'stage' family … you suddenly have a son, or a daughter, which you don't have in real life. Maybe you wear a crown, maybe you are bowed to and are applauded as you walk into a room. It is a form of escape from the tediousness of your own existence. However Ellen was finding her own way, she had given up living in other people's shoes because her own life was now more exciting than playing a character in some playwright's work, and being at the mercy of critics, your agent and the public. Some actors act to forget themselves, but if your own life is so exciting, you may find wearing other people's shoes not quite enough even if you are wearing a crown.

CHAPTER 14

▼

The phone woke me up next morning and I wondered who would be calling at this early hour.

"Hullo?"

"Nicole, good morning. It's Joan."

"Joan, good to hear you. What's up?" I hadn't seen her since we got back from Blue Harbour.

"I was up early, so I thought I'd let you know our news. John and I are going to Australia for six months. Charlotte doesn't want to leave her course at Drama school, so we are leaving her here. John has been offered Higgins, you know, the Rex Harrison part in 'My Fair Lady' on a six month tour, then he will see what kind of film work there is out there. It will be good for both of us as we really want to miss another English winter if we can."

"Well, that's a surprise. When are you leaving?"

"Next week. I should have phoned you before but things have been happening fast around here."

'How's Edith?" I asked.

"She's fine. That's one of the things that we are pleased about when we had to make a decision. She has settled down well and enjoys the company of the other old actors."

"I'll go and see her if you like."

"Oh, would you? She'd love that. Charlotte will be going every week, but it would be lovely if you could too."

"Of course."

We chatted on for a few more minutes, it was clear that she was very ambivalent about going. However she said she wouldn't want John to be out there for six months on his own and he had heard that there was lots of film work for Brit actors out there.

"You'll come back with an Australian accent, I bet."

"Not bloody likely."

"It's very easy to pick up."

"When John went to get his visa to work out there, the chap asked him in all seriousness, if he had a criminal record and John quipped ... I didn't know I still needed one." She gave me their contact number and rang off.

As I hung up the phone, I realized there were two more people going on to live their own lives, admittedly John in the shoes of Professor Higgins, for six months at least.

When did the idea come into my head about living my own life? It was a rationalization of course. I'd rather be playing Nina in 'The Seagull' than digging in the garden at my little French cottage bought in a rash moment. Or would I? Everybody seemed to buying places out of England, either Italy, France, Portugal or Spain. I wondered why I wasn't so tempted. Perhaps because I was alone and I couldn't think of anything more boring than drinking a bottle of red wine, watching the wonderful sunset in my own little house with no one to talk to, and nothing to do except watch telly, or surf the net.

CHAPTER 15

▼

I decided to have a dinner party for Ellen and Ian before they left London so I got up and started cleaning the flat. It had been ages since I had done any real cleaning, just a 'lick and a polish.' I started with the kitchen deciding that the shelves could do with a cleaning and some new paper. It was such a boring job, no wonder I hardly ever did it. Taking out all the piles of plates, cups and saucers, glasses, bowls, vases, coffee cups and mugs, then putting them all back again, on the fresh paper.

Just as I was in the middle of trying to fit the paper around the cupboard door Tony called.

"I've just had a call from a chap at the Henry Irving Society who are having a fund-raiser-cum-evening reception and they had asked if you would consider doing your one woman show about Ellen Terry for them. It would be paid of course. It's good money."

It seems some of the members had requested seeing it again. I was flattered and cheered, as I hadn't done the show for ages, even though I had been such a success.

It brightened up my day and little did I know that the evening would be so eventful.

The story of Ellen Terry's life is remarkable. She was not only the leading actress of her day acting of course in Henry Irving's company and being courted and admired by George Bernard Shaw and many others, it was how she handled her blindness and old age which was truly courageous. I played to a captive audience and the applause was warm and generous. Afterwards at the reception an attractive woman about my age came up to me and introduced herself. So I met

Dianne Coldstream. She chatted for awhile and asked if I would consider doing the show on board the Cunard liner, the Queen Elizabeth 2. It sounded very interesting and she asked me for lunch to discuss it the next day.

Ellen woke me up with more wedding plans. Should they have a small orchestra, or just a pianist for the reception?

"Oh you must have Michael Law and three or four of his musicians fly out", I said without hesitation. He has to be the best. Take Ian to see them here and he will agree.

Michael Law plays all your favourites, remember?"

"Of course!" I'll call him. Thanks a million."

"What could be better than Michael Law on the rooftop of the Danieli overlooking Venice?"

I didn't tell her about the meeting with Dianne. Later, perhaps. She was too involved with all her plans.

"Oh, Nicole, I'm so happy … everything is going so well. There is action, after months and months of inactivity, waiting for the phone to ring, waiting for that big break, I can tell them all to go to hell."

The lunch with Dianne went on for over two hours. We found so much in common to talk about. First of all I was rather curious about what she thought of the show.

'It was great, very entertaining and informative. I never knew all that about her. The story of her life is very moving and profoundly sad.

However it was Dianne who I found profoundly interesting. After two hours I was in awe of her.

"I was a librarian in the north of England for many years and one day I booked myself a holiday on board the Q.E.2."

"Travelling alone?"

"Yes, I had no one to ask to go with me. A librarian's life is not a very social one!" she smiled.

"During the voyage, I went into the library on board to borrow a book and was surprised to see how few books they had. They had the usual Charles Dickens of course, and some Naval books, old magazines and some very old novels. I felt so frustrated especially as I had been keeping my own library very up to date, that I sat down and wrote a letter to the Cunard Line telling them what an unsatisfactory library they had."

"Good for you!"

"Sometime later I was surprised to receive a letter back. I've forgotten exactly what they said. I had obviously told them I was an experienced librarian, but the gist of the letter was that I was welcome to try to make it a better library!"

"Good heavens … it must have been a good letter!"

"Papers and contracts crossed back and forth. I was invited for lunch to discuss the details and then I was given a free hand. I loved it."

Now, five years later she has her own company, a staff of five, an office, a warehouse and the libraries on ten other ships.

She was so modest about it, as if it was nothing at all.

The waitress brought more coffee even though the place was almost empty.

"Please go on", I said.

"So then I suggested to the powers that be, that bookshops on the ships would be a good idea. To sell the latest best sellers, ship's posters, souvenirs etc. I applied for the concession to be able to run and operate them. I formed a second company and recruited a sales staff and a land staff."

She spoke as if it was like ordering daily delivery of milk.

"As well as ordering books for the libraries?"

"Yes."

"How did it go?"

"It was really hard work, carrying all those books on board. We had to move down to Southampton."

I sat there in awe. I was listening to a real entrepreneur, a clever business woman who was bringing literature to places where it had never been before. Making a ship a centre for literacy, culture, reading and even CDs.

Further ideas came tumbling out and I sat there listening. She had even further plans ahead which involved more ships and more books.

"I also adore opera", she said. "I try never miss Glyndebourne, or the Covent Garden season. She was au courant with singers, composers, directors, scores and of course the operas themselves. She had her own opinion of many different directors. She had already made plans to go to Italy and France to hear two new operas and then she would be going to open an office in Miami because the cruise ships she wanted would be based there during the winter. She would also have to find staff and a warehouse and find a wholesaler for the books.

"That is amazing!" I looked at her slim figure and soft red brown hair and decided she looked like a young Deborah Kerr.

"But I want to know more about you", she said.

The waitress came to fill up our coffee cups once again but we both waved her away. It was probably a hint she wanted us to leave.

"Well I'm very depressed at present. No work." I shrugged.

I hated the way I sounded, so pathetic really, after listening to her conversation.

"Acting is very frustrating because you usually have such long periods of unemployment. It is a waiting game and I think I've almost had enough of it."

"Oh, but you are so good. I saw you in the film that you won the Oscar for", she smiled.

"Ah yes, what a circus that was!"

I was tempted to tell her that the movie cost me Michael, the love of my life, but resisted. I was curious about her private life, but would have to wait till later for that information.

She was also a theatre buff, and knew about the legendary actors.

"That's why I was at the Henry Irving Society's event."

I was suddenly transported out of central London by her. She was like a breath of fresh air. Sea air rather, with visions of a wide blue enormous ocean … white cliffs, seagulls wheeling overhead, the deep resonant sound of a liner leaving a port.

I had always imagined those big ocean liners were the epitome of a luxury life. First class staterooms, first class stewards looking after your every need, handsome Captains, those sexy ship's officers in their white and gold uniforms, gleaming Art Deco bars, exclusive restaurants, exquisite lounges, black-tie dinners, elegant women, masses of flowers in your cabin-and of course the sea.

Noël Coward again! He loved sailing in ocean liners and the shipboard life. He wrote song 'Sail Away' and travelled many times by ship.

"When the storm clouds are gathering in your sweetheart's eye … Sail Away, sail away"

Dianne must have sailed in ships too many times.

"I think your world must be very exciting" she said. Echoing my thoughts exactly. "Creating characters, rehearsing, the first nights, the audiences, the sound of the curtain going up, and then Hollywood and the Oscars!"

I loved her version of show business. Of course there are the down sides to everything I guess. But right now, her life looked a lot more fun than mine did.

We both looked at our watches, we were both surprised how the time had flown.

'Why don't we go across the road and have some afternoon tea? I have a meeting later but we can keep talking till then."

She took me to a little place that had a small garden outside where we sat at a wrought iron table under a tree. Only someone like her could find such a place in central London.

We continued on about books, plays, operas discussing all our favourites.

'Where do you live?" I asked.

"Just outside Oxford, in what we call a little 'close'. Three small stone cottages facing a small square with a high wall protecting the property from the outside world. My mother lives in one cottage, our office is in one, and Paul and I live in the other."

I was to see it later in the year.

This lovely lady was offering me work. I was being given a new lease on life. She was throwing me a lifebelt.

Now I was going to be like Ellen, live another life even if it wasn't for ever.

We spoke of her work as a librarian and her love of books, then of the hours upon hours she spent ordering books for the ships.

Eventually we parted and as I walked home I realized I had found a new friend, a wonderful imaginative friend who wasn't in the theatre. Whose life was totally different.

Someone who could possibly lure me away from acting into a new career. I loved my books, especially the ones I have read over and over again. I read most of the books that were in the Sunday Times Review.

Tony had left a message that the Society had called to say how much they had enjoyed my performance. That's nice of him. Wait till I told him my news.

Next day, Dianne called and said she had found a date for me to go across to New York on the Q.E.2, during which time I would perform my show and also do a poetry reading on another evening. I love people who get right back to you, immediately, who don't talk about 'in a week or two'. She then said "And I'd like you to work for me. "Work?" the word sounded fabulous.

"When you get back, we will have another meeting and I will tell you what I have in mind."

I couldn't imagine. I had already offered to be one of her librarians on board to help check out books to passengers but she had some other better idea. My mind raced ahead. Now the whole world opened up. What about all those other ships? The ones that go to Australia with stops on the way. Ports like Pago, Pago, Fiji, Tahiti ... Hey, all that is Somerset Maugham territory ... British colonials like Mr. and Mrs. Edgeworth and settings for Coward plays. I wondered if I would go over there with the show.

Ellen Terry, what are you doing for me? Do you think Ellen spirits stay with actors who are still searching for work? Ellen felt so close to me when I was working on the script of her life. If you think about a person deeply enough can they help you? I thought about Brian and wondered if he had any idea about this thing. Obviously he had been very depressed, maybe too much so, to pick up any spirit world. I didn't want to get so desperate that I would contemplate suicide. You just try to hold on. If you are beginning to crack, get out. I was ready.

Coward had gone off on sea voyages after all. He traveled the world and needed new horizons to conquer.

The dinner party went off very well. Just the three of us. I told them about Dianne and they were very enthusiastic, especially as they knew how much I loved the sea.

CHAPTER 16

▼

Ellen came over the next morning, for a post mortem. She wanted to talk more about Ian of course. As I helped her off with her coat I noticed she had on a new dress I hadn't seen before. It was a double knit in white and navy stripes, very French.

"Lovely dress", I said.

"Yes, it's Ian's choice. He loves to go shopping with me."

I would have been envious any other time, but now things had changed.

"All the arrangements had been finalized. I think we are all set." She smoothed down her hair after taking her scarf off.

"What are you going to wear?" she asked.

"I haven't decided yet … do you want me to buy something new?"

"No not really. Why don't you wear that beige lace gown with the low back … it is so dressy, and put a big rose in your hair. That will do. It is so dressy I don't know why you bought it."

I went into the kitchen to put the kettle on and she followed me in.

We talked about Dianne and her achievements.

"Boy, some people have all the luck!"

"Was it luck? Or was it the power of networking? Imagination, initiative, vision, you make your own future. You have to seize every opportunity."

"There is nothing sadder than a missed opportunity."

"If I hadn't done that reception then I would never had met her. Imagine. Just shows you as the songs says … what good is sitting alone in your room! Come to the Cabaret."

Ellen smiled at my lousy singing.

"I envy you going to New York again … however I wouldn't want to be there now without Ian", she said.

'Well I won't have much time there, because they give you two nights then you fly home … unless you pay your own way. Besides, I feel like you do, I don't want to be there on my own."

"You never know, you might meet someone on the ship, silly!"

"I doubt it. One in a million chance."

"My cousin met the First Officer on a cruise and married him … mind you it didn't work out, she found out he was married to the sea, not her."

"So many of them are, I guess. It is a calling after all, just like the theatre."

"Well it's stopped calling me. Thank goodness."

She continued …

"However, I have been thinking of creating a theatre company in Venice once we are married." She suddenly announced.

"What?"

I smiled and reached for the teapot. It was empty so I got up to refill the kettle.

"Seriously. I have to have something to do. There must be lots of Brits and Americans living there who would support me." Or Italians who want to hear English being spoken."

"Great. But get the wedding over first."

"Of course."

"Have you told Ian about your idea?"

"Not yet … but he won't mind."

"Why not a cabaret room? Then you could hire musicians who don't have to speak English."

"That's an idea."

"You wouldn't need to do any rehearsing, you could just hire them, promote them, then sit and enjoy the show.

'There maybe dozens of cabaret rooms there."

"I doubt it!"

"Let's go shopping! Liberty's has a sale on. I want to buy something nice for Ian. Then we will walk down to the Ivy, have lunch and see who's there!"

As we walked along Oxford Street I suddenly realized how shabby it had become. The old dress shops that used to be so fashionable had gone, the road was bumper to bumper with buses, and everything looked very tatty. I wonder how many streets in London would begin to look the same.

I was already thinking of the wide open ocean which I hoped to see in about ten days time.

CHAPTER 17

▼

I'd just got into bed, and switched out the light when the phone rang. Who could it be at this time of night?

"Hullo", I mumbled.

"Nicole … is that you?"

"Yes!" The voice sounded familiar.

"This is Charlotte, Charlotte Spencer … remember me?"

She sounded awful.

"Yes, of course. How are you?" I knew something was wrong. Oh dear, I hoped it wasn't about Joan.

"I'm not very well actually," She started to cry and couldn't speak for a while. "I'm sorry Nicole but I'm very upset." She certainly sounded it.

"Where are you?"

Between the tears, she managed to say "I'm at the Sloane Square police station. I've been arrested and I need someone to come and get me. It's a long story but I don't want to call any of my friends or any of Mum's friends, except you. It is so horrible, I thought you would might be the only one who will understand and maybe help me. I was going out to see Mum and Dad in Australia next week, but they have taken my passport so I won't be able to go. Please can you come and get me?"

"Of course, Charlotte. I'll be there in 30 minutes. Goodbye, I'm on my way."

Oh dear, she wouldn't tell me what had happened on the phone so it was still a mystery as to what happened.

I pulled on some clothes and hailed a taxi. It wasn't as late as I had thought. On the way over I wondered what had actually happened. Drugs probably, but she didn't see the type. I had got to know her quite well at Blue Harbour and she seemed a rather serious girl intent on her career and very fond of her mother and grandmother. They will be devastated I'm sure when the news gets out.

As I walked into the Police station I saw her seated on a bench at the far end of the room. She got up and came over and kissed me.

"Oh thank you so much for coming ... I was scared you wouldn't be home."

A police woman came over to me and made me sign some papers for her release, then she said something that shocked me ...

"Blackmail is a serious offence. She could go to jail for a long time you know. You will be responsible for her and she is not allowed to leave the country until she appears in court."

"I understand. Can we go now?" After the woman had given back Charlotte's purse, her watch and stuff from her purse we walked out into the night.

"You'd better come back to my place tonight ... unless you want to go home. Is there anyone there?" I asked.

"No, not now. The police were there this afternoon. I really rather go back home if you don't mind as they made such a mess searching the place. I'm starving and I know there is some cold chicken and salad in the fridge. Will you come with me?"

There was little I could say. Besides I wanted to know what had happened. She was still very choked up and couldn't stop crying. She said she would start at the beginning when we got back.

"Oh thank you for coming ... you have no idea how I needed you. I have been in the police station nearly all day."

As I paid off the cab she let us in. The house was an old brick place just off Holland Park with a small driveway and a garden squares on either side. Joan had sublet the top half of the house to a teacher who was away at present according to Charlotte.

We went into the living room and I noticed that all the drawers in the bureau had been left open and the place was indeed a bit of a mess.

"They made me stand in the middle of the room while they searched the whole place ... it was awful, they went through every room. They found my passport and took it."

"What were they looking for?" I queried.

"Proof that I was blackmailing others."

"What?"

"They were looking for letters or something ... I don't know ... come into the kitchen and we'll eat. Would you like a drink after all this."

"Please help yourself, it's there on the counter."

The food was on the table in no time flat.

She opened a bottle of wine and poured it into large glasses.

The story came out very slowly she was still so upset.

"It all started last week. I answered an ad on the Internet for an actress to audition for a play which was being produced by a new company starting with try-outs out of town. There wasn't much information but as usual I sent out my photo and resume. I still haven't got an agent so I sent my address here. A few days later I got a letter saying I had an audition Thursday, which was yesterday. The audition was at a hotel near Sloane Square which I thought was a bit funny but as I knew that some people hire suites for business meetings, and if wasn't upstairs in a hotel room, that it would be O.K. When I got there, it was indeed in a small conference room on the ground floor. There had been some meeting there earlier, as there were cigarette butts everywhere and half empty bottles of water, maybe the same people, but there was only one person there. He said the others had left as they had a train to catch as that I was the last to audition. He said he was the producer. He seemed quite nice, well-dressed for a theatre person I thought.

A bit creepy, but that's usual.

I poured some more wine as she continued.

'Well, I did my audition piece and he really seemed to like it. He asked about my future plans would I be available from certain dates … the usual stuff. It really seemed as if I'd got the job because he wanted me to see somebody else, the actual director, the one who would be finalizing the casting. Then he said that he had to vacate the conference room by 5 p.m. so he would wait for him in the bar. Would I join him because he wanted me to meet the other guy. It all sounded legit to me."

She looked exhausted and I wondered what was coming next. I helped myself to another piece of bread and butter, I was hungrier than I thought. We were too stressed out to think about sleeping.

"We went into the bar which was pretty deserted. I ordered a glass of white wine and he went over to the bar to get it rather than wait till the waiter came over to take our order. I noticed he sat beside a huge bowl of flowers, almost hidden from me. I went to the bathroom to freshen up. When I returned he said he hoped the chap wasn't going to be late, because he too had a train to catch. I then began to feel really, really hot and flushed and I asked him if we could sit outside in the lobby which seemed a lot cooler, as I had crossed it on the way back from the ladies room. He took my glass and followed me out of the bar to a table in the lobby. I felt really strange, sort of drunk but not really."

I put my feet up on the chair next to me to wait for what was coming next. I kept thinking of Joan and how upset she would be. No wonder Charlotte hadn't wanted to call family friends.

"Well, to cut a long story short, Nicole, he had drugged me and all I remember is him pushing me into a cab and me telling the cab driver my address. He took my keys from me and came into the house. He said we needed another glass of wine, and why didn't I put on some music so we could dance. He put more of the drug in my glass because the next thing I knew was ..."

"Was?"

She began to cry. "Was when I woke up in bed this morning."

"What ... you remember nothing?"

"Nothing ... I looked in the other bedroom to see if he was there, but he'd gone. I examined the beds, to try to find out if I'd been raped or not. It was horrible. I was in a state of shock. I was terribly confused I walked around in a daze. The drug must have still been in my system because I felt really weird. I took a hot bath and washed myself all over. Then suddenly I felt angry, very, very angry. I couldn't find my glasses. I'd just paid over two hundred pounds for new prescription, bi-focal glasses with expensive frames and they were gone. They must have fallen off in the taxi. Then I missed my locket ... the one Dad had given me. It was a gold locket on a gold chain ... I had been meaning to get a more solid chain for it as it was too fragile, but that must have broken in the taxi as well. I can remember I tripped and nearly fell when I was pushed into the cab by him. It was a struggle that seemed strange at the time."

"How awful."

She went on and things got worse ...

"I found his letter with his phone number on it. Thank goodness the police had missed it. Naturally he didn't answer, but I left a message saying it was urgent that he call me. Then I phoned the police to report him. He called back shortly, as I guess he was curious. I was in a rage by this time and told him about the loss of my glasses and my gold locket, my head was hurting, I felt sick, and I went on and on. Then I told him I wanted him to pay for them. I didn't know what to do. The police sounded so indifferent. I asked them would they please come over and check the place out but they said for me to go into the nearest station and file a report. I wasn't well enough to do that and I was too angry. So I said to him 'I want you to pay for my glasses and locket. Meet me at the same hotel at 11 a.m. and bring me five hundred pounds, or I will go to the police'. He sort of screamed out then and said 'No don't do that please … all right I'll meet you at 11.am. It was only about 8 o'clock then so he had plenty of time to go to the bank. I felt a little better. At least I could replace my glasses but not my locket. However, little did I know but he then also phoned the police and reported that he was being blackmailed and if they would come to the hotel at 11.am they would catch me asking him for money. I didn't know this of course, otherwise I wouldn't have made sure the police had my report first.

Well, the police planted a microphone on him and when I met him and asked for the money, it was recorded. I spoke to him and told him it was a wicked thing that he had done and where was the money?

He said he had the money out in the car, and as we walked out through the lobby a police woman came up on one side of me and said 'You are being arrested by the police … you either come quietly or we will handcuff you.'"

"Oh God, what did you do?"

"What else, but go with them? I was perfectly calm, because I thought I was in the right. He would be punished. Little did I know they had recorded me, and had the statement from him. Back at the police station they took me into a room and asked me to tell me what happened which they recorded. Then they brought me back here, God knows why, to search to see if I was running a business black-mailing men, for heaven's sake! Then back to the station until they had got more information and charged me. Then I called you. But you know they didn't get Mum's number because I said they were in transit to Australia. Thank God. But I'll have to tell them."

"Yes, but not now." I was appalled. "Do you think you could sleep? It's been a long day."

"You are so kind Nicole. Thank you so much. You know it is dangerous for young actresses to seek work. I realize that now."

"But it wasn't your fault", I tried to reassure her.

"I read about this date rape drug, but never thought it would happen to me …"

"It must happen to a lot of girls … that's why I am shocked at the police's reaction. They must have been suspicious, but I guess it was because he got to them first."

"I wasn't well enough to go down to the station. You know they say that certain drugs stay in your system for ages and they can affect your judgement and rational thinking."

I made a mental note to look these drugs up on the Internet next day to find out more about them.

Finally, we changed the sheets on the beds. I took the guest room, and we fell asleep quickly without any further talk. We were both shaken up and she was totally washed out.

She unplugged the phone as she didn't want to have any kind of disturbance during the night.

Next morning she was feeling a little better and I really didn't want to leave her. We had coffee and toast in the kitchen.

"I have lots to do today, Nicole, so I'll be fine. I realize I will have to tell Mum and Dad because I'm going to need a lawyer and I guess they can recommend one for me. If I play it down a bit they may not worry."

"But surely, the lawyer will tell them you have been charged with blackmail."

"I'll ask him not to until after the court date to see what happens."

I took a cab home and decided not to talk to anyone about it for Charlotte's sake. She promised to let me know when she had to go to court.

How vulnerable young actresses are especially in large cities. Ambition and fame are the spur. They will endure almost anything. I wondered how Joan will react.

Charlotte called next morning and said she had talked them, telling them the whole story. Joan was flying back the following weekend.

"She said to thank you for all your help, Nicole. She was going to phone you, but I said to wait until she gets back."

"That's fine."

I told her about my new the job and she thought it was great.

"At least it will be a new adventure, Nicole."

"I hope a pleasant one."

CHAPTER 18

▼

Before I left London, Dianne and I had lunch again, she wanted to tell me about the other job now, because she might be away when I got back. She told me that she would like me to find actors like me who perform one-man or one-woman shows, to find actors and directors to do small cast plays and classic anthologies for the ship. To organize a theatre company so that there would be some alternative entertainment on board, rather than just the casinos and showtime spectacles. Of course, I knew so many actors who had their own shows, and who would be perfect. I was delighted with the offer.

The day came for me to board the ship. There she stood in the dock. Rather than go directly up to the gangplank which was upstairs, inside the terminal building, I went down onto the pier outside, to take a photo. Walking below, looking up, the hull was huge, standing out of the water. As big as a skyscraper almost. She was big, black and beautiful and a strange kind of excitement seeing such an enormous vessel ready to cast-off for far away places on the high seas, hit me in the stomach. I was going to be part of it. The bustle of the porters, the shouts of the deck hands holding thick ropes, the seagulls swooping down to get a better look. There were huge containers being loaded on board, probably caviare and steaks, I thought. I smiled in expectation, and glowed with the anticipation of the voyage.

Most passengers had boarded before me, so I missed what I heard was a huge line-up. A steward greeted me at the ships' entrance and escorted me to my cabin. Why does the idea of someone escorting you to your cabin sound rather over the top? Such service. However I had to get used to it because you were waited on hand and foot during the voyage.

After unpacking, (I hardly had any clothes at all) I went to find the Cruise Director's office to say I was on board and I that I had received the Welcome Package they had left on my dressing table. They gave me a few more instructions and asked me to a cocktail party after we had sailed.

It seems I would be doing my show the next evening after dinner. So off I went to look at the theatre where I would be playing and made arrangements to meet the lighting director the next morning for a run through for the lighting cues. Small time for them as I noticed their huge lighting board and special effects keyboard, that looked like they could do a production of Star Wars if they'd wanted to. I could have played Ellen Terry on a space ship I'm sure. Special effects and all. Worth thinking about? It might give the show a new twist.

Then came the boat drill when we all had to find our life jackets and go to the deck to find where we all were to go if there was an emergency. We were allocated different lifeboats and I'm sure everybody was thinking of the sinking of the Titanic as they were listening to the Captain's announcement from the Bridge. However he then told some Monty Python kind of jokes too cheer us up, including instructing us not to flush the toilets all at once, because no matter what we thought, the ship wouldn't go any faster.

Dinner time was an interesting experience. All the guest lecturers and people who taught Bridge, watercolouring, languages and such met at the party beforehand where we all chatted politely, then we found we were all sitting together in the dining room. Some asked if they could sit on their own, especially the couples, so we split up soon after. Maitre'D asked if I'd like to sit at the Captain's table.

"He won't be down this evening. He never comes on the first night out, but should be here tomorrow."

Well, why not? 'I'm sure he orders great wine', I thought.

However, it was difficult to think of conversation and questions about the ship that he hadn't had dozens and dozens of times before. It turned out that his wife was an actress, had been at the same drama school when I went there, but I couldn't remember her. She was acting in the play 'Habeas Corpus' in rep and we both knew the script, so could repeat some of the funny lines which Alan Bennett had written. That was fun.

He told me about a Broadway composer who had been at his table on the last voyage. The producers had phoned him and said they needed two new songs a week for their new production.

"Come on Al, it won't take much out of you", they said.

"No, but it will take a lot out of Bach, Beethoven and Brahms."

We seem to have more laughs than the others at the table which was slightly embarrassing at times.

Next evening the show went very well. The audience did seem to enjoy it, although I admit some went to sleep. The sea air, I expect. Well at least I hoped so.

Then I met Natasha. She came backstage after the show.

"I loved your Ellen Terry. Just a wonderful show", she said.

I looked at her, as I wiped off my make-up. She was a petite blonde, rather plump, about ten years older than me, maybe more. And American, rather like Lucille Ball. She sparkled as she spoke. It reminded me of that saying: that there are four different kinds of people in the world-the twinklers, the sparklers, the drones, and the worthies. She was definitely a sparkler. Glamorously dressed in a black strapless gown, with a black velvet ribbon around her neck, with a diamond brooch in the centre. Very chic I thought.

"Do you feel like having a drink to celebrate?" she smiled.

"Yes, that would be lovely." I looked around, nobody else had come backstage, so I presumed everyone had filed out of the theatre.

We walked down to the nearest lounge, some people passing smiled, others said "We enjoyed your show!"

After she had ordered some champagne, we started to talk and it was just a little like meeting Dianne for the first time.

"I was an actress in New York. My first job on Broadway was understudying Katharine Hepburn. However, she went on to describe her present life, which was not in the theatre-although theatre of a kind, when you think about it.

"I travel alone, now. After three marriages I've had enough."

"But you are so beautiful", I replied.

"Nothing that special. But I was in Europe with a singles group and all the men were so old and decrepit I didn't want to go home with them, so I came on this ship instead."

"Where's home?" I asked, 'where do you live?"

"Most of the time in Manhattan, but I have four houses in the Hamptons plus a nightclub and a place in Palm Beach", She said in a matter of fact tone of voice, as if she was telling me she had four cats and a dog.

I'd never heard of the Hamptons. It sounded vaguely like the Cotswolds. She filled me in. "Out on Long Island, on the ocean is where everybody goes. There are great beaches as far up as Montauk which is on the end of the island.

"The Hamptons are about 100 miles out of the city. It's where New Yorkers go in the summer, to get away from the city heat. I have three houses in Hampton Bays, which is also where the nightclub is, then I have my own place in Southampton. Do you play tennis?" She asked.

"I used to, but haven't played for years."

"I love the game. My ex-husband was a great player."

Then she turned to me and asked: "Surely you are not travelling alone on the ship?"

"Yes, I am. I wanted it that way. I decided to tell her about Peter and his death. "So you see, it's too soon to think about anyone else"

"Sorry, I shouldn't have asked" she said.

We chatted on about what roles she had played including her favorites. When she mentioned Amanda in Coward's 'Private Lives', I told her about the visit to Blue Harbour.

"Sounds incredible! Especially if his pianos and books are all still there. What songs he wrote! Even though his plays and films are wonderful, it's those songs that are so unique. Who else could have written 'Mad Dogs and Englishmen' and 'Don't Put Your Daughter on the Stage Mrs. Worthington'? They will last for generations to come!"

I began to relax after the show, The champagne helped, as did her high spirits, and the relief that people seemed to have enjoyed the evening. Now, more people knew about the life of Ellen Terry and her world which was very satisfying.

We got up and said goodnight, making plans to meet tomorrow for lunch around the pool. Then I went out onto the deck, which was deserted, and stood at the ships' rail looking out at the dark sea and the waves below splashing along the ship's side, which was lit up by the ship's lights, so the sea foam looked white in the night.

We were going very fast and it was hypnotic looking at the water rushing by. There was no moon but I thought I could still discern the horizon way off. Standing there was so romantic I suddenly wished I had some man to share it with. Peter and Michael were both gone … would I ever meet anyone else I could really love?

I thought of Brian and his suicide, he must have been thinking about doing it for sometime, otherwise he wouldn't have had such a huge prescription for sleeping pills. If he could have compromised, realized that maybe he didn't have the genius of Coward, but could do something of his own whether he became famous or not. But he wanted fame and he knew he would never achieve his ambitions so he just didn't want to live anymore. I've always thought people who live on their own get weird eventually, just because they become so self centred and self-obsessed. Hey, enough!

It was getting cold, even though the scene was so classic, all that was needed was some Wagner playing to set the scene.

The ship was rocking slightly by the time I got down to my cabin, so when I got into bed it was like being rocked in a cradle. Very pleasant, as I listened to the creaking of the ship which even sounded like a wooden cradle, maybe I was going to find a new life, or at least a new career.

CHAPTER 19

▼

Jogging round the deck next morning to try and get rid of extra pounds I knew I had put on, there was a stiff breeze blowing and it blew away all the cobwebs in my brain.

The ocean stretching way ahead and way behind, the wide sky seemed higher than in England. You felt part of the Universe, the air was so invigorating, the sky so high and the clouds even higher. There really wasn't anything quite like it. I could well see why Coward loved ships and the sea.

I went to the 11.o'clock lecture about space travel. 'Who could ever afford to go there, I wondered, 'And what is wrong with what we have here?,I thought,looking out at the view through the ship's window."

At lunch, Natasha educated me into the class system of New Yorkers, and their pastimes. It all started with the 400 Club. They were the most wealthy and influential people in New York and every thing they liked to do was recorded. The Club was supposedly meant for only 400 people but it soon grew until it had to be disbanded. They started going to the Hamptons, joined private Clubs, learnt how to play tennis or croquet. Gave parties and balls and made their daughters into debutantes. It took an insider to tell me the rules of the social game.

"Yes, we have our aristocrats here too you know", she laughed. "The Brits are masters at snobbery but it exists here too, especially in the Hamptons."

"First of all are aristocrats, who go back a long time. Now we have the old families who are still in Southampton and Palm Beach and there is a social register to tell you who is who. The Meadow Club in Southampton, is the posh club and they have so many grass tennis clubs it looks like Wimbledon. When the mist is coming in from the sea and the tennis players, all in white are still playing it is like something out of a novel, or old film. It is poetic. You will see their croquet courts and the club house is something that should be in a Scott Fitzgerald novel. Then we have the Bathing Corporation just a few yards from the Meadow Club, on the ocean, where if you want to swim you can use their large swimming pool or go into the ocean. If you don't belong to these clubs well, what can I say?"

"Where do the people come from?"

"Mostly New York, but many from across the States"

The poolside buffet was marvellous … She had taken a chicken and avocado salad, I had salmon salad, stuffed vine leaves, pesto pasta and pine nuts. We watched the not-so-slim swimmers getting in and out of the pool. That should have stopped me from putting any food at all in my mouth but I thought that it was only for 5 days, and I'd diet next week.

The desserts were so numerous. Cheese cakes with many different toppings, mint chocolate cake with strawberries on top, glazed apple and peach tart with blueberries on top. Ice creams included nut-filled vanilla, chunky chocolate chip and peanut brittle, caramel and coconut, not to mention apple charlotte, crème brulee and eclairs.

I passed on all of them, storing up calories for dinner time.

She seemed to have taken a great liking to me and I could feel she would be a really true friend. I felt that she instinctively knew so much about many things. A bright woman, who I discovered had a flare for real estate and bargains of all kinds. Later on I would discover her secrets.

"Why don't you delay going back to London for a few days and come and stay with me for a few days out in the Hamptons? We can drop some stuff at my apartment in New York. I'll pick up my car and we'll drive out to Southampton. You'll love it out there, it's just like England, snobs and all."

Then she told me what happened last night.

"There's a man at our table who has been chasing me and after we had a nightcap in the lounge, he walked me back to my cabin. We walked the entire length of the ship, along the thick carpet in the corridor, it must have been a few hundred yards. We were arguing all the time about why I wouldn't go to bed with him. I kept saying "No! No!" He kept on and on. "You only live once", etc. Finally, when we reached my cabin door, we heard a little giggle from behind, and some woman had been following us all the way along the hall and had heard everything. As she passed, she smiled and said,

"Sorry but I heard the whole thing."

"We just didn't see her, that's all", she laughed. "We waited for her to comment, but she just went on walking passed us."

She said he had nearly convinced her, but not quite.

"He is really not that attractive and I'm not that desperate!"

I thought she was charming. When she invited me again to go with her to the Hamptons, I accepted.

"Why not? It will be a new experience. I like having guests!" She smiled again.

"Why not, indeed." It would be an invitation that Coward would not refuse I thought. He used to visit people upstate and outside New York, all the time. In fact, one of his plays was all about his experiences in such a place. I remember he met such interesting people on his sea voyages, making friends or re-meeting old ones on board. His diaries were full of his being entertained by colorful characters, who sometimes put into his plays.

I couldn't make up my mind if Natasha was a socialite, per se: she seemed to be much too busy to devote much time to superficial social events.

"You need better clothes", she said.

"I noticed your dress last night. That's O.K. for Ellen Terry, but you will need more for Southampton. Come on, lunch is over. Come down to my cabin and we will see what I can find."

Funnily enough, walking down the corridor we passed the guy who had propositioned her. She nudged me and said "Guess who is coming towards us?"

He looked very nice and I told her so.

"Not for me, old girl."

"Hullo again", she said as we passed by him. "See you tonight!"

I got a whiff of after-shave. It was Peter's brand. Oh dear, I felt faint with the sudden recognition. Proust-like, it immediately brought back all the pain I had been trying to suppress. Thank goodness Natasha was ahead of me and didn't see my face. 'Yes, Natasha', I thought. 'Yes, I want to be with you to have lots to do and new experiences so I can get on with my life. So what if I lost all the continuity in my life? The acting world could do without me, thank you very much'.

There were hundreds and hundreds of actresses sitting in London who would say and do the same thing, if they had the chance. The ones who had given up their private lives, and family for their career were still in doubt if it was worth it. I wished that I would have had a child, but it wasn't too late, maybe it will happen.

"Come in, and close the door!" Natasha's cabin was larger than mine and the steward had been in to tidy and make the bed. She went to the closet and started taking out clothes.

"This would look good on you". She held up a pale gray cocktail dress which was pulled across on the hip to a sequinned star on the side.

"It is too long for me and I can't be bothered having it altered. I don't know why I brought it."She put it on the bed.

She continued to go through her wardrobe and gave me some rather lovely clothes. "Take them, I've got much too much here but I never could decided what to leave behind. Remember we were travelling in Europe for three weeks."

She had as many clothes as a fashion editor might have brought. She reminded me a little of some business tycoon looking around at her luggage, fur coats and the jewellery she was wearing.

I contacted the Cruise Director and he made the contact with the offices on land who changed my flight till a week later.

"No problem", he winked.

Oh Christ, he thinks I'm off with someone!I sighed.

"Thanks you so much. I'm going to out to the Hamptons with my girlfriend." So much for him I thought.

I looked forward to visiting a new place with my new found friend.

Remembering vividly that Coward often went off suddenly and did something competely different from his normal life. One of my favourite songs of his after all is "Sail Away"

"When the lovelight is fading in your sweetheart's eyes…. sail away."

He knew the advantages of change, of travel, of some exciting new place, usually with witty, social people who entertained him, that sometimes had nothing to do at all with the theatre. New horizons, new friends, new ideas.

CHAPTER 20

▼

We docked at 8 o'clock in the morning. It was great coming into New York Harbour. I had brought a copy of Coward's diaries with me and he had described the same thing. We passed the Statue of Liberty and went into New York Harbour which was a total thrill. We had to wait until all the regular stuff had been done before we got onshore. We got a taxi across town to Natasha's apartment and went upstairs.

It was on the East Side. "The place to be!" she said. Her apartment was full of antiques, lovely paintings and masses of bric-a-brac. She showed me around the place and outside on her spacious terrace, where all the furniture had been covered over.

"New York is so dirty, you have to clean every day especially if you have outdoor furniture", she said.

I helped her unpack and hung up some clothes for her in her huge closets in the bedroom.

"My goodness, you have a lot of clothes Natasha!"

"What did I tell you? Take anything you want."

Again, I was amazed at her generosity. I had been given enough already.

Her bedroom had a lovely big bed with a canopy over it.

Very theatrical, with drapes to match on the windows.

She called downstairs and asked the doorman to get someone to bring up her car to the front door. 'How New York', I thought. 'How convenient.'

We had a quick look around, then she locked up the apartment and went downstairs. The car was waiting. It was a snazzy little sports car.

What a drive! I was terrified! Sweet Natasha was a lovely person, but what a driver! She drove like a maniac. She was all over the road and talked to drivers who got in her way.

I decided that perhaps this was the way I was going to die.

"Do we have to go so fast?" I asked.

"Yes, we have to beat the rush hour traffic, otherwise it takes hours. Don't worry, I know the road I do it all the time."

"Have you ever had an accident?" I tried to be diplomatic about it.

"Not so far."

I tried not to distract her with any conversation but she wanted to talk.

I noticed she had a number of talking books on the back seat and she said she played them all the time when she was alone. "When I drive up from Palm Beach they help with the long distances." She lifted her left hand off the driving wheel, to show me a scar. "Last year I had an operation on this hand because I had carpal tunnel syndrome. I had to drive up from Florida with one hand."

My mind boggled.

"Didn't really bother me, as I had the talking books to keep me company. I listened to Homer's "Odyssey" last time."

We stopped at her three houses in Hampton Bays, which were side by side to each other in a semi circle. She checked the interiors as she was going to rent them for the summer.

"I brought out a box of china and some lampshades, but I need a couple more."

We continued up the highway, then turned off into a side road. Suddenly she came to a screeching stop. There was a sign. 'Yard Sale'.

"Yard Sale?" I asked.

'Yes, I stop at most of them. Come on, let's see what they have."

"But aren't we going straight to your house?" I was exhausted and felt like a wrung out dishcloth.

"Soon … I always stop on the way."

She bought a dresser!

She had two men put the top down on the car then put ropes across it with the dresser on top.

"I need this for the second house, it is just the right size!"

We eventually made it to her house, after doing some grocery shopping at a supermarket in Southampton first.

Later that weekend one of her friends told me that Natasha had actually lost a dresser, and the drawers, on the highway, when driving out a few weeks earlier.

The friend had been a passenger. "When we got there, the dresser had gone. It had fallen off and was somewhere in the middle of the Long Island expressway."

As Natasha was staying out there for ten days, I accepted a ride back to New York with her friend at the end of the week. Her driving seemed to be her only weakness.

That evening she invited several guests to dinner to the famous Meadow Club. As we walked along the wide veranda leading to the front door of the old wooden club house, I noticed all the grass tennis courts laid out in front, beautifully manicured and ready for play. Like something out of 'Vanity Fair' in the 1920s. The front hallway had glass cases full of silver trophies, cups and plates all inscribed, with various medals as well. There were framed photographs on the walls as well, of former members and winners of tennis and croquet matches. Just like Hurlingham in London.

We went into the bar for pre-dinner drinks, everybody seemed to know each other and then we all went into the dining room where a small orchestra was ready to play for dancing. The buffet was laid out in a side room and there was as much choice of entrees and desserts as there had been in the ship.

At our table, we had a doctor and his wife, two widows who were known to be great hostesses, a well known New York jewellery designer and a retired Air Force Colonel. Plus Natasha and me. The men followed the standard etiquette of asking every woman around the table to dance, presumably because they all could dance. I wondered if Americans were all so cultivated, being able to play tennis and to be smooth ballroom dancers as well. The evening progressed with people coming by the table to say hullo, and I knew that I had been recognized by several of them.

Louis Jordan, that handsome actor who played opposite Leslie Caron in 'Gigi', was sitting at the next table, and he nodded in recognition, which was nice.

"What is the Colonel's name again?" I whispered to Natasha.

"Bill Watson", she replied, as she got up to dance. Bill and I had been left alone at the table as I was having trouble with my new high heeled sandals and didn't really want to dance the tango.

"Your career sounds fascinating!" he said. He had seen my Oscar-winning movie. I was surprised, because he must have been about 20 years older than me, so his tastes would be different.

"I drive my lady friends to movies they want to see out here, also to dances and dinner parties."

I had met my first 'walker'! Men who accompany women as partners, socially, with no sexual overtures or commitment from either of them.

"There are so many widows out here", he continued "that we are in constant demand. They pay all the expenses. If you own a tuxedo, drive carefully, dance well, don't get drunk and tell a few jokes, you can have a wonderful life out here."

"But surely you must get bored?" I asked.

"Not at all. These ladies are very interesting. They are rich, and often I call them by their fortunes. For example, Wednesday night I am escorting Mrs. 'Listerine' to a ball, and the next night Mrs. 'Johnson and Johnson'. Their husband were very bright men, so they don't suffer fools gladly. They have seen it all and when they go out, they arrive early and leave early which is fine by me. I'm usually back home in bed by 10.30."

I enjoyed talking to him as he was so entertaining, he was witty, charming with a twinkle in his eye. He had been widowed ten years previously so had bought a house out here shortly afterwards, near the Meadow Club and had about three invitations a night to go either elegant mansions, or balls or the private clubs.

"I like chasing younger women, of course", he smiled at me, "But like dogs chasing cars, if I caught up with them, I wouldn't know what to do with them!"

He told me about his career in the Air Force and how he had been Head of Protocol for SHAPE in Paris, looking after VIPs from the Pentagon, when they came to visit. He had a suite at the George V, as well as a penthouse suite at a second hotel for entertaining. He gave cocktail parties too, it seems, to return the hospitality of the hostesses. So he had an ease with people and a certain flair for always having something interesting to say, if there was a lull in the conversation. He seemed curious about my career and asked me lots of questions. I liked him a lot. He reminded me a little of Michael in his interest in life and people as if he still wanted to be part of the universe.

When we got home Natasha said laughingly, "Well you certainly made a hit with Bill! I've never seen him sit out a dance before. You know he is a big hit with the heavy furniture set out here?"

"Heavy furniture set?"

"Yes, that's what he calls them. The widows. He is the no.1. walker in Southampton."

"I can see why. He is very entertaining."

Next morning, we went over to the Club to play tennis. Natasha was a good player and she had asked Bill and his friend to play with us.

"What a serve!" I said as Bill smashed one across the net.

"He must be 70 at least!"

"Nobody knows"

I hadn't played for ages so they really creamed us, with Bill at the net and Natasha more of a 'hit and giggle' player.

We all piled in the car and drove over to the Beach Club … There were all the same people there, sipping drinks on the patio. "Hullo, Hullo, Hullo", said Bill as he worked the patio, shaking hands all around.

"He's so popular. He remembers everybody's name and he networks like crazy, introducing people to people who he thinks should meet each other. Look at him now, over there! He is taking that couple over to meet those newcomers from England."

I watched him before he came over and sat down with us.

"Why don't you and Natasha come out with me for dinner tonight? What are your plans? I know a cute place in Sag Harbour. You should see as much as you can before you leave this area."

I looked at Natasha.

"We'd love to Bill, thank you. Where did you have mind?"

"Oh it's a new place. I will surprise you."

"Good. About 7 o'clock then?"

We went into the club house for the buffet–again, wonderful choices. I have never eaten so much lobster and salmon. It was abundant here. Lovely salads, which you don't see much of in London.

After lunch, Natasha and I headed for the beach and Bill went home for his nap. "The only way I keep going", he said.

The surf was quite strong and we loved jumping the waves. I felt like a teenager. 'How can I go back to London after all this', I thought. I might grow tired of it, but I was suddenly in a totally different world. These people could not only produce plays on Broadway, they had so much money, but probably build new theatres and cultural centres around the country if that is what they wanted to do.

Back to reality. How could I possibly fit into that world, even if I had wanted to? I was lucky to have seen the social world out there, but it was too rich for me. There definitely was a class system, and theatre people were accepted–just. They were tolerated. There were a few famous ones with houses out there, but they were not really in the social circle. George Plimpton lived in East Hampton which was entirely different. The artist and writers lived there and were nick-named 'zazoo's' by some of the snobs.

We drove out one night to an Art Gallery opening which I found fascinating. Lots of celebrities there and I knew some of them. But I was beginning to feel restless. Next morning I finally phoned Ellen.

"Nicole, where are you? Thank goodness, you called. I've been trying to reach you. You are not answering your e mails and I didn't have a phone number for you. The wedding has been postponed." However, she sounded cheerful.

Good old Ellen … couldn't wait for my answer as to my whereabouts. I could have been in a hospital somewhere, who knows?

"Oh no!" I said. "Are you all right?" At least, we knew that she wasn't in a hospital somewhere.

"Yes, I'm fine. But the good news is I've got the lead in a new play at the Royal Court! It's a fabulous part. We start rehearsals next week!"

"But what about Ian? What does he say?" I sensed danger for her. A warning. Oh God, please don't let the same thing happen to her. She risks losing him as I did Michael making the wrong decision.

"He's fine with it. He says he'll enjoy being a 'backstage Johnny', and that we can easily postpone plans till after the play is over."

"When will that be exactly?"

"They don't know yet. If it is a success, we could extend the run. When are you coming back?"

"On Wednesday. I stayed on another week. Sorry, I meant to call you. I'll see you sometime Thursday. Have you signed the contract yet?" I hoped I might be able to talk her first.

"Yes, it's all signed and delivered. Don't worry. We hadn't sent out the invitations yet, so all is well."

"That's something. I suppose."

"Must go now, call me when you get in."

I put down the phone in shock. Natasha came into the room.

"Is there anything wrong?" She saw my face.

"Oh, that was my old friend Ellen, in London. She has postponed her wedding to a great guy because she has be offered the lead in a new play."

"Obviously another actress!"

"Yes. She's had a difficult career, waiting for the big break, you know. Well, now she seems to have got it."

"Are you pleased for her?"

She looked at me as if my answer was important to her.

"I'm just very surprised, that's all. She was adamant about giving it all up. When she met Ian, she was sure of it. They had planned their wedding in Venice, she was going to invite all her friends, and now she has decided to stay in London and continue her career."

I had told her of course, about my decision to go to LA on my own and what that cost me in personal loss.

"I know what you are thinking, Nicole, but maybe Ian is different?"

I shrugged. "I don't know really. We both want her happiness, but I can't help feeling that she is making a mistake."

Natasha laughed. "There is always a cost, no matter what, especially if you are working on a creative project. Other people don't appreciate what you do and so often have no idea what you sacrifice for your work. It is just the nature of the beast."

I listened to her account of her personal worries about her husbands and children, and knew she was talking sense.

I thought of Joan and how she gave up her career because of John and his illness.

Even in this critical time, when I had to decide if I wanted to act again, it made sense to listen to Natasha.

"I found the price too high". "Besides," she smiled, as she bit into a blueberry muffin, "I inherited a great deal of money, and having a success in the theatre didn't seem that important anymore. I didn't feel like shouting, either, which of course you have to do onstage every night. As the saying goes … living well is the best revenge."

She was right.

Next day, after she insisted of giving me some of her jewellery and more clothes, I packed, then waited for my ride back into New York and Kennedy Airport.

CHAPTER 21

▼

Arriving next morning, in the rain, I went straight home, anxious to hear what had happened to Charlotte, Ellen, Beryl and Jane. I had had no news since I left two weeks ago, except the phone call to Ellen.

The flat was dusty and stuffy. I opened all the windows, watered the plants and checked the plumbing. I inspected the contents of the refrigerator. Nothing had turned green, although the milk had turned sour. I flipped through the mail, nothing interesting, mostly bills and bank statements. Two cards wishing me Bon Voyage and an invitation to some new play opening in Soho of all places.

I called Charlotte and Joan answered the phone.

"We've been to court once, but everything was postponed because of various procedures. I thought it would be all smooth sailing but it is not. So we have another date next week. I feel badly leaving John but at least he is working!"

"Charlotte was back at school, but still shaken up," she said.

In fact, Joan was trying to talk her out of going back to drama school and into giving up the idea of an acting career entirely.

"Well, just have to wait and see. But I hate leaving her here. I hope she will come out with me."

Next, I phoned Beryl. What a surprise and it was all good news. The play would be done next month, she had met Jane and they got along famously.

"She's like the daughter I never had", laughed Beryl. "We are inseparable and she is going to play the housekeeper in the play, believe it or not. My life has changed enormously, Nicole, thanks to you. I couldn't imagine in all my dreams, that this could have happened. If only Brian had lived."

I agreed, thinking that we never do know when life throws us something good, totally unexpectedly, without having to think about it.

But now to Ellen. I'd left her till last because she was going to be more difficult. I was still capable of being hurt by her intense feelings, so I decided not to advise her, even though I had the worst feelings about her relationship with Ian.

He was such a nice bloke. All for the Royal Court!. What happens next? "What's Hecuba to him, or he to Hecuba? That he should weep for her?" How can an actor be more devoted to a role, a character, on stage, than to one in real life? Ask Hamlet.

She wouldn't be advised. "I know what I'm doing, Nicole. It was different for you and Michael. He was a different kind of man. Ian is far more mature and understands completely."

She wanted to know about the trip and the visit to the Hamptons, so we arranged to meet for lunch.

"Where is Ian now?" I asked.

"He is down in Morocco, arranging to sell his house down there."

'Morocco?"

"Yes. He thought he might settle there, but he's changed his mind."

"Didn't you want to go with him?" I would have jumped at the chance, I love couscous and Moroccan food, but I didn't want to sound critical of her decision, whatever it was.

"Not really. He was going to have a week of business meetings, so I would have been on my own in the house with nothing to do, except to show prospective buyers and that wouldn't have been much fun. Besides I'm not mad about Moroccan dishes. That's all they seem to eat."

"Maybe he has a Moroccan girlfriend down there? You never know!" I liked teasing her.

"Nicole, that's not fair. Why do you say things like that?"

She took out her lipstick and small mirror and did her lips. It is something we both felt essential. If you weren't wearing lipstick, you were somehow not dressed completely.

I told her about doing the show on the ship, about meeting Natasha and staying in Southampton. She wanted to see the clothes she had given me and the jewellery.

"I can't imagine her giving you all those things. She must be a truly,amazing lady", she laughed.

"Just like a fairy godmother, really. I found her such a sympathetic friend. But then, most Americans are. They're generous in spirit, very hospitable and usually very open minded. You really have to know someone personally to actually discover this."

"Well, she sounds a real sweetheart. I would like to meet her someday. Perhaps Ian will take me out to the Hamptons when we go to New York."

"Oh? You didn't tell me you were going to New York." I turned to look who was coming in the door, as there was some kind of disturbance. It was a group of tourists demanding a better table. They were terribly dressed in cut-off jeans and tee shirts with the usual backpacks.

Honestly, surely this restaurant of all places, must still have a dress code. But, alas they don't. I watched as they were led to a better table near the door. I decided I wouldn't come here quite so often anymore. The place was going downhill fast.

"Yes, eventually we will go because Ian still has family in Canada and we will go up there through New York." She was watching the group also with disdain.

"I couldn't imagine going out looking like that", she said.

"We wouldn't even travel in a bus like that. Surely they must know what they look like?"

"They don't care, that's all."

"Actually it was the same on the ship. People would go to the Captain's cocktail party, then go back to their cabin and change into tee shirts, and go back up to the dancing, when most people were still in their tuxedos and formal dresses. The staff turned a blind eye. So you had some one in braces, dancing next to someone in a formal tuxedo."

"Yuk. Crass, I'd say."

We walked back to my flat to have coffee. On the way, we bought some flowers at the flower market. We both missed not having any. When you are working in a play, there seem to be flowers all the time, so we cheered ourselves up by buying some huge white lillies, roses, pink ones, purple irises, peonies and baby's breath, thinking of Virginia Woolf's 'Mrs. Galloway' when she wanted to buy the flowers for her party, herself. We buried our noses in the blooms to soak in their perfume.

It started to rain so we ran the rest of the way, laughing as I hurriedly unlocked the front door. We had forgotten to take umbrellas. A foolish thing to do in London. I opened the door and went into the kitchen to find a vase for the flowers, and put the coffee on.

We went into the bedroom and I showed her the clothes that Natasha had given me. As I took them out of the closet, and laid them on the bed, she couldn't believe it.

"They're beautiful, Nicole!"

"I know. I would never buy anything like them for myself. Besides I wouldn't be able to find anything like this to buy." I held up a chic black evening dress with straps criss-crossing across a very low back. "Where would you find something like this?"

"Mmm. Maybe in Harrod's, but at a very stiff price."

"And this?" I showed her the gray cocktail dress with sequinned star on the side ...

"Well now, you have all this great stuff. Where are you going to wear it? I don't see your social calendar is all that full with dinner parties and soirees at the Garrick Club, for example."

"It is just so unusual to meet someone like her and see the kind of life she lives. Clothes are obviously her passion. You should have seen her closets, both in New York and Southampton. Absolutely enormous with rows and rows and rows of clothes."

"Well, I might become like that too!" Ellen laughed.

"Never!"

"Who knows? You say Natasha was an actress, wasn't she? When she stopped working, maybe she became a shopaholic."

"I tell you what, when Ian comes back, why don't we really get dressed up to the nines, and go somewhere posh?"

"Where would that be exactly?" I was curious.

"Oh, I don't know! Let me think about it. Maybe to Annabelle's?"

"That place is so dark. Nobody can see what you're wearing, let alone even see you, if it comes to that."

"Well, we will think of someplace. Surely there is someplace in London where you can still go and see well dressed people?"

"Maybe Ian will know of a place. He gets about so much."

"In the old days, not so long ago actually, you could always go to the Savoy and dance in the River Room, but all that has gone now.

The phone rang. It was Ian. I handed the phone over to Ellen. "I know, I've been out all day with Nicole. But you are a clever chap finding me here!"

It turned out that the sale of the house had fallen through and he would have to stay on another week, to see if they could find another buyer.

"Oh, never mind!" said Ellen. I'll have started rehearsals by then. Maybe it is better that he stay there, because it will be a hectic week. You know what the first week of rehearsals is like. Besides I will have to study and learn my lines, which is always time consuming."

"Tell me about it" I said, putting back all the clothes in the closet.

"When do you open, exactly?" I wanted to know in case I decided to take off somewhere on the spur of the moment with my new trunk of clothes!

"Three weeks from today, actually."

"Great! I'll be there. Beryl's opening in next week, so maybe you'll be free to come and see Brian's play?"

"I'll try to. Depends on how rehearsals are going. I can't imagine that it is finally being produced!"

"Beryl arranged it all. I've never seen someone so absolutely determined. It is a lesson to us all. Never give up. Persistence is all that matters."

She went to the mirror to comb her hair and check her make-up.

"You mean money. Money is all that matters. She would never have done it without Brian's money."

"Never mind. Whatever it is. She is to be congratulated. I really admire her as she had so little experience in these matters. Let's hope the critics like it."

"It is a tiny bit old-fashioned, you know." Ellen had read it as soon as she heard about it. Naturally looking to see if there was a suitable role for her.

"But it is all about a time that is past, like Proust, or Moliere. The story is eternal. It's just that manners change."

"Society changes. You know I watched a movie on the telly the other night, that was so disgusting that it sickened me. I don't know why they allow such scenes to be shown."

"Don't get me started Ellen, you know that's my pet peeve."

"O.K. Point taken. Let's change the subject."

I took out the photographs I had taken at Blue Harbour. For some reason Ellen had not seen them, and as I passed them to her I looked at some of them and realized what a wonderful trip it had been. I thought of what Joan had told me about her giving up her career for John, but now it must be doubly difficult because she was here in London and he was in Australia. At least he was at the theatre every night, although she must wonder what he is up to afterwards. She thought of Edith, who not only had to worry where her actor husband was, but whether he was with a man or a woman.

At least Joan did not have that worry, or at least if she did, she hadn't mentioned it.

We both went to Beryl's first night. She looked wonderful in the foyer greeting people, and this is where we caught up with her. I prayed that it would be a success, a critical success for besides all the money she had invested in it, I thought it was a good play. I recognized many theatre people there which was an encouraging sign.

Ellen had been at rehearsals all day, but dashed home to change and get 'dressed up' as I had ordered her to. Even if we were the only ones who were in evening clothes, to us, it was a mark of respect for Brian and Beryl. There were several others we were pleased to see, even though there were masses of blue jeans and sneakers as well.

"Oh there's, you know, what's his name? The one who can't even find his way over Waterloo Bridge to get to the National?"

"Hullo and good evening to you both!" Beryl came across to us. "Thank you for coming. You do look glamorous!" Looking us both up and down.

"You know we wouldn't have missed it for the world!"

We air kissed each other.

"Are you very nervous?" I asked, looking at her troubled eyes in a calm face.

"Yes, a little. I'll feel better after it's all over."

"Well, we'll go in as the foyer so crowded. Break a leg!"

I wondered if I should have stayed and talked to her longer but there was really nothing much to say. Only time would tell.

"Hullo, you guys!" said a voice behind us. We turned around.

It was Stephen, an actor we both knew from way back but hadn't seen for ages.

That's the great thing about show business. You have so many friends, even though you may not see them very often, it is like old home week when you do. Actors you have worked with, often for months so that they become like your own family. They end up knowing you better than your own family does because they see you for the better part of the your waking hours. You experience the same physical and emotional highs and lows, the work, the stress, the laughs, then the curtain falls with the audiences applauding and you feel the love and appreciation pouring over the footlights for a job well done.

It's difficult to get the same adoration at home sometimes. Therefore, there is usually a bond between actors who have worked together, though not always, and they enjoy seeing each other again and catching up on news, even after several years.

"Hullo, Stephen. Where have you been? What have you been doing?" He looked well and was wearing a nice suit. It was the usual chat about plays, and directors and reviews.

We stood talking as people pushed past, then found our seats which were down in the front.

The theatre was full. We looked up at the balcony, where we used to sit as students. It was full too. There was a buzz in the air. A first night is always pretty exciting.

The lights dimmed and the play began. We held each other's hand in a tight grip. I looked for Beryl but couldn't spot her. She was probably going to walk up and down at the back of the dress circle, the usual place for playwrights, producers and directors on a first night, if they haven't gone down to the Embankment to pace up and down there to contemplate the murky waters of the Thames.

The first laugh! A round of applause for the leading lady's entrance. Good sign. Good audience.

The second laugh, even louder. We held our breath because this is the make or break time. The time that the play starts leaving the ground or it sinks. You listen for that first deadly cough from a member of the audience. It is the death knoll and starts the whole chorus of disaster. It is psychological, if only that stupid coughing bitch knew. It breaks the spell which the actors are weaving so carefully. Just as bad as the ring of a cell phone.

It is ironic to think that the playwright, directors and actors are at the mercy of how the audience feels that night. It could be compared to an animal. It can be in a good mood or a bad mood. Each night is different. No one can tell, except perhaps if an audience is particularly noisy just before the curtain goes up, it means they are excited, some of them in high spirits coming from the bar or a cocktail party and are in the mood to enjoy themselves. And so it was that night.

There had been quite a few articles in the papers about Brian's suicide, so people came out of curiosity, as well as to see the play. Brian had worked as an actor for a number of years, so lots of his friends came, Stephen being one of them.

At the interval, by the time we got to the bar, it was almost time to go back to our seats. Stephen bought us some drinks, we shouted across to some other friends we saw, to say hullo. People were smiling, but the noise was deafening, so we couldn't hear any kind of remarks about the play.

Stephen liked it, that was important, because we admired his work and he was quite influential in the theatre world.

How we wished Brian was there. The second act went as well as the first, laughing together with that whole audience was a joy. These are the things you remember. The whole house laughing as if in unison. There was a roar of laughter as the last line was said, as the curtain came down. Oh what relief. They liked it! Ellen and I looked at each other and grinned. The applause was great. Lots of curtain calls, then Beryl walked on the stage. Suddenly the whole audience fell silent. A deep hush as she walked across the stage to centre stage. Her speech was brief and to the point. Ellen and I were close to tears as we looked up at her.

"Ladies and gentlemen, thank you all for being here. I am the playwright's sister and I just wanted to say that I am sorry Brian is not here, although I am sure he is in spirit."

"Oh, dear", I thought. "She looks as if she's going to break down." But no, she took a very deep breath, raised her head slightly, and continued.

"As you all probably know, Brian was in the theatre for many years before he started writing this play. He had it rejected many, many times, and became discouraged to the point he just put it aside deciding to leave London and the theatre. He died in Jamaica. It wasn't until after his death that I found the play and managed to have it produced. I just want to say that theatre people should never give up their dreams, dreams that sometimes require courage and persistence, but often are the only reason for living."

I looked at Ellen. There were tears streaming down her face, as there were on mine. Beryl was being so controlled, so brave, so determined.

It was astounding to see how much she had changed. Changed from a timid woman to a strong woman full of life and purpose.

She made a few more remarks and ended by thanking the brilliant cast, the director and the audience. Again, lots more applause, then the curtain finally came to rest.

We were overjoyed. Looking across the emptying seats, we saw people smiling as they filed out. We waved to Stephen, he waved a 'thumbs up' sign to us. He knew I had been in Jamaica when Brian died.

"If only Brian could have been here." Ellen whispered. She was still choked up about Beryl's speech.

I pictured him as I last saw him. Sitting in the dark at Blue Harbour, with the moon on the water, the wind blowing through the palm trees, and talking about Coward. However this was his night tonight, and I knew he had been here.

CHAPTER 22

▼

Next morning, I threw on some clothes and went up to get the papers from the local newsagent. The reviews were all good except for one, which isn't worth mentioning. They were unanimous in praising both the play and the actors. It was a hit. I don't know what we would have done if it hadn't been. It was just not worth even thinking about, it would have been so horrible.

Ellen called and asked if I had seen the reviews. She hadn't bought all the papers so I read them to her.

Next I phoned Beryl who had read all of them of course. We had seen her backstage afterward and also Jane, who was very good in the play.

I hadn't seen her for ages. She gave me a big huge hug and said she owed everything to me. I think she had moved in with Beryl at this point, and they had waited up together for the reviews. Well, what a relief.

I decided I would get dressed after sitting in the kitchen for well over an hour, reading all the papers. As I walked out into the hall, the phone rang again, this time it was Joan.

"Hullo Nicole, how are you?"

"I'm fine Joan. Thanks for calling. How are you?"

"I've just been reading the papers. I see that Brian's play was a success last night." she said. "I'm so pleased for Beryl and for Brian."

"Yes, it was a wonderful night. Beryl made a little speech after the curtain calls and she was really marvellous. It's just amazing how that woman has come out of her shell. I guess just a bit of success gives one confidence."

"Was it a good house?" she enquired.

"Packed, and I hear the bookings are going well too. Now after the reviews it should run for awhile."

"That's great. She worked so hard to get it on, she deserves it."

"You must go and see it", I said.

Joan had phoned to invite me out to their place for Sunday lunch. It would be just the three of us and Joan wanted to cook a roast lamb.

"Yes, I'd love to come. What time?"

"Say about one o'clock?"

"Fine."

As I was on my way there, I realized I hadn't seen Charlotte since she had called me that night from the police station, so I wondered how she would be.

It was a lovely day and their front garden was full of flowers.

"Greetings!" Joan smiled. "Come on in and we will have a drink out in the garden."

I walked through the house, remembering that awful night. The living room was tidy and well kept, not like the night I saw it. It was really a lovely house, and as we went out to the larger garden in the back, I could see the wisteria vines gracing the terrace and the veranda.

'What a perfect day, isn't it?' I felt very welcome. It was such a pretty garden with an ornamental fountain at the end of the long lawn. Everything looked well cared for, and I thought how pleasant to live in such a lovely place.

Charlotte came out and gave me a hug and sat down in one of the wicker chairs. She looked well, even though they were going through such a terrible time.

I knew they wanted to talk about it and after a delicious lunch, when we kept off the subject they filled me in.

"We went through a nightmare last week. You know that police woman never believed Charlotte's report and when we went to court, she really tried to have Charlotte sentenced for blackmail. For a time, it was touch and go. Charlotte would have gone to prison!"

"Oh, no! How could that be? The woman must be mad!"

"She doesn't like me", Charlotte said.

"No, it's obvious", said Joan. "She doesn't like Charlotte at all. Maybe it's plain jealousy, or you know, sometimes people just don't like the way you look or how you comb your hair."

"What happened eventually?" I was shocked.

"They postponed the hearing again. Our lawyer said he wanted more time, so they agreed on another hearing next week. Nicole, I'm so scared. The judge seems to be on the side of the police. They think because Charlotte is studying to be in the theatre, that her morals may be questionable. I just can't believe this is all happening. And even more, that police went and searched the guy's house, and they actually found some more of the drug he used. But when questioned, he said he had it prescribed by his doctor for his insomnia, and he only used it when he couldn't sleep! Yet still the police believed him and not Charlotte. The police woman actually said to her 'I'll see you in jail'."

"How terrible. Have you told John?"

"I had to, because I thought I'd be flying back at the end of this week. He feels awful that he is not here to help but what could he do anyway. I'm thankful it hasn't been reported in the papers. I'd hate Edith to find out and someone would be sure to tell her."

"How is she, by the way?"

"She's fine. That is at least some consolation. I am here for her when she thought I'd be in Australia. We go out to see her at least once a week. She is well taken care of there."

"I'm pleased to hear it!"

"There are so many of her friends staying there. They talk shop all the time. It's interesting to hear their anecdotes about all those old timers. There were so many of them whom she worked with. She can watch her old films, which she does with the others watching too, so that cheers her up."

After I had left them, on my way home, it occurred to me how actors are still regarded in some circles as gypsies. Well maybe we are, but that is harking back to the days of the Victorian era, when being an actress was regarded as being little more than a whore. I wonder when we will gain respectability? We have to give a good example I suppose, to people who don't know any better. Take that police woman, she must have it in for Charlotte because she is so pretty and slim, and has perhaps a glamorous future ahead of her. But to disregard Charlotte's report was so unjust.

As I was leaving, I tried to be as helpful as I could,

"Get another lawyer to advise", I suggested. "Someone who may be able to find a different approach or has more influence."

"Yes, we are working on that now. We had a consultant lawyer brought in yesterday."

I felt I wanted to go out and visit Edith. Not because of Joan and Charlotte but just to see her. Often talking to an old pro does wonders. They have done it all, experienced all kinds of heartbreak and usually have very sound advice, especially with regard to personal matters. They don't mind talking about their past careers, because there is nothing really to hide at their age so you often learn a great deal. Biographers know this, of course.

Time flew by and Ellen's opening night was drawing closer. As usual, there were the usual tensions, between other actors in the cast, the director, the stage manager and the playwright. I got the blow by blow account almost everyday, until at one stage, I thought they might not open at all.

In the middle of this Ian phoned from Morocco with the news he had broken his right leg and was in the Tangier Hospital. It never rains but it pours, as Proust once wrote.

Of course, Ellen was beside herself, not only worrying about the opening but who would take care of Ian after he got out of hospital. He was only in there for two days so they could watch to see if the metal pin they put in was bothering him.

"Oh, Nicole, I'm so worried about him. I am certain he must be in pain and I'm not there to help. It's as if the Gods are punishing me or something!'

She was very emotional and upset, which I thought was very bad at this time, especially as she had to conserve her energy for her role.

You have no idea how much physical energy is necessary for a stage role. It looks so easy, but your whole body is working. Projecting the character, using the voice, controlling your breathing, your movements, even though it looks so natural. It is exhausting, physically hard work. Some actors don't survive because of it.

"Do you want me to go out there?" I asked.

"I don't know, I just don't know. He says that he has friends who can help him and get food in."

"He'll probably need a nurse to come in each day. How is he going to wash and change the sheets and do the laundry?" Ever the practical one, I had to point out all these things to her. However, even after meeting him once, you knew that he was capable of organizing everything. He was just one of those kinds of men who could take charge. Money helps, of course, you can get people to clean, cook, wash, shop and he had enough funds to do all that, as well as stock up with good wines, some champagne, some merlot, a pot of caviar, or pate, maybe even order a hamper to be sent down from Fortnum and Mason, if Tangier didn't have what he wanted. He just must have been a bit pissed off that the woman he was planning to marry wasn't with him.

"Just concentrate on the play. There is nothing else you can do. You don't want to mess up after all your work."

To me, I think that was the turning point in their relationship and she knew it too. He needed her and she wasn't there for him. He must have realized that if her career was to continue, that he would always come in second place. He just wasn't that kind of man I thought. He needed more, a soul mate who could enjoy the finer things of life with him, travel with him and be there for him. He was a traveller, an adventurer, and therefore how could you possibly have a career of any sort if you lived such a life. Maybe a travel writer, maybe not. Certainly not a hard driven, ambitious, editor-in-chief kind of woman. But then, those types perhaps wouldn't need a husband anyway.

Again I sat through another opening night. Ellen wanted me to go to the dress rehearsal but I wanted to see it sight unseen, so to speak, on opening night.

"Darling, you were marvellous!" I meant it, as I went backstage afterwards. She was. The play was awful, boring and pretentious, but she made it come to life with her incredible vitality. I was very impressed. We went to the party afterwards where I met up with some of the company from Stratford, old friends and the camaraderie of catching up with their news, was warming. In fact, I seemed to be having a better time than Ellen, who looked tired and wanted to go home.

She knew she had been good and now they were all just waiting for the reviews as usual. I said goodbye and followed her out.

"I'm really tired, Nicole. Let's go before I pass out. Ian said he wanted me to call him whatever the time, so let's go. Tomorrow is another day."

'Yes, you're right." I had no idea of the surprise that tomorrow would bring.

CHAPTER 23

▼

Next morning, as usual, I jogged up to the news agency to get the reviews. Not very good. The Times hated the play, but liked Ellen. The Daily Telegraph hated it too. Oh dear. But Ellen got a good review from nearly all the papers.

I called her. She was pleased, but obviously upset about Ian and that he hadn't been there. All their plans seemed to be falling apart. The house should have been sold, he would have been back in London, but it wasn't to be. She said she wanted to go back to sleep so we said we'd talk later in the day.

Five minutes later, I was having coffee in the kitchen and waiting for a piece of toast to cook. I love Tesco's thick brown wheat for toasting. Together with thick marmalade it is almost my favorite meal of the day. The phone rang again.

"Hullo?"

"Hullo, Nicole, this is Nigel."

"Nigel?" I was at a loss for a second or two.

"Yes, Nigel Fox, from Jamaica. Remember?" He laughed and waited for some recognition from me.

"Nigel. Of course! I'm sorry. I was miles away."

"Well yes, Jamaica, is miles away!"

"Of course, I remember you. Where are you?" I asked.

"Here in London", he said. "I know I should have written to you, but it was a last minute thing. I didn't really know I would be coming until a day or so ago."

I remembered that lovely voice. He should have been an actor. His voice was that good.

"I meant to phone you, too. But things were hectic before I left. How are you?"

"I'm fine, thank you. How are you?" I thought of how handsome he is. Yes, I will see him if he asks me.

"I just arrived last night, but I was wondering if you would be free for dinner tonight?" He sounded so terribly nice. I remembered his smile, among other things.

"Yes, I am free, as it happens", I laughed.

His voice brought back such pleasant memories immediately. I felt a butter-flies in my stomach, not that this was abnormal under the circumstances.

"Where shall we go?"

Well, I thought, maybe he will fall in love with me over grilled onions.

"Why not Rules?"

He'd never been there before. So I had to tell him how to get there.

"I'll make a reservation and see you at 7 o'clock. Is that O.K?"

"Fine. Looking forward to it."

I was too.

"What's your phone number if I can't get 7 o'clock?" I asked. He gave it to me.

"I'm at the Dorchester."

"Well, that must be nice!" I laughed.

"I used to stay here years ago, but it has changed considerably. "So what else is new? I would have loved to have made a reservation for the Savoy, but that is now dead and gone as far as elegance and class is concerned.

"We can go on to the Savoy", he said. A mind reader too!

"Let's see, shall we?" I said goodbye and hung up.

Now, how am I going to tell Ellen? I wondered if I should call her and tell her now. No, she was sleeping.

It is going to be very tricky, because she is so upset about Ian. If there was any-thing I could do for her, I would do it. Maybe I could call Ian, and tell him to get back here even if he had to take an ambulance to the plane.

"No, stay out of it", I argued with myself. But she is my best friend, I have to do something. Someone had to save the day. Time is changing everything, and things are not going to be all good in the future for Ellen.

I wondered if I should tell all this to Nigel. Would he be bored? It was fore-most in my mind, so maybe he would have some suggestions or advice. But he'd never met Ellen or Ian so that didn't make sense.

Then suddenly I had an idea. Why not, indeed, call Ian and suggest he get an ambulance to the plane. He could get doctor's care in London, he probably would be on crutches by now, so he could get around a little. I thought it would be the only solution for her. He could stay at her place, or at a hotel and be with her. The more I thought about it the more it seemed the right thing to do. I would have to get his number from her. But I wanted it to be a surprise for her so how to get it. I'd think of something.

I felt better, now that I had a plan.

Beryl called to say that the play was a great success and the bookings were going well, also that she and Jane were very happy together and they were thinking of going into business together.

"What kind of business?" I asked, quite surprised at their initiative.

"We thought we might open a shop."

"What kind of shop?"

"A little antique shop."

"But there are hundreds of them in London", I said, slightly disappointed that their idea wasn't more original.

"Only, this one would be different. We would like to specialize in theatre memorabilia. A Theatre Antique Shop. We'll go to auctions and buy things from the estates of famous actors and actresses, and collect playscripts they had used with their notes in the margins, programmes and posters. That kind of thing."

"That sounds great" I said.

She continued, "Also you know, there are many actors who paint and draw quite well, so we would take those too, on commission of course. They are often very good. I visited an actor last week who had done some portraits of his friends and they were very likeable. Besides Jane loves going to auctions."

My mind boggled. Not only was it remarkable that Beryl had come out of her shell and become a well groomed, cheerful, resourceful woman, but that Jane had followed in her footsteps was also a surprise. Thinking about the first meeting with Jane, I was dumbfounded that she had ever been to an auction, let alone bid and bought anything. Wonders never cease!

"What is the deciding factor for you both, whether to go ahead or not?"

"The actual location and rent for the shop. We think we have found a place, we are just negotiating now."

"I hope it works out. It sounds like a lot of fun!" I really felt pleased for them.

"Thanks, Nicole. We owe you so much. We wanted you to be the first to know."

Well, that was a piece of good news at least!

Later that afternoon, I called Ellen. She was up and about, feeling much better.

"Listen Ellen, I'd like to send Ian some flowers."

I wasn't making it up, I really did want to send him some.

"You don't have to do that, Nicole."

"No I really want to. To cheer him up. So give me the address where he is, and the phone number."

"Well, if you really want to." She gave me his address and telephone number. So that was easy enough. He was sure to be home because he was a semi-invalid.

First of all, I sent the flowers so that he would have them the next day. Then I had to decide when to call him. Maybe just before I go out to dinner I thought, then I wouldn't sit and brood if things didn't go well. I somehow thought that they wouldn't.

I dressed with care. It took about 30 minutes, after trying on three or four things, to decide what to wear. Good old Natasha had saved the day. I chose the gray with the sequinned star again. It was to turn out to be my favorite and I wore it over and over. It's funny how we can wear some thing far more than something new we bought to replace it. I had so many dresses hanging in the closet that I never wore. Just didn't feel comfortable or there was a button off, or the zipper needed repairing.

I carefully applied my make-up, using the minimal amount of eye liner. Those heavy lines are so dating, I think.

Then I was ready. I dialled Ian's number. He answered right away.

"Hullo, Ian. It's Nicole, in London. I wanted to find out how you are."

"Hi there, darling. How are you? Good to hear from you!"

His voice sounded cheerful, as always, a deep resonant voice with a slight Canadian accent.

"We are really worried about you. How are you feeling?"

"I'm fine. Just a bit boring here in bed all day. The doctors say I have to stay still till the bone starts to set." Then, sensing that I, instead of Ellen, must have a reason for calling he said, "What's up?"

"Well, I know you know all about Ellen's opening night last night and how badly she feels about not being there with you instead? I just had an idea Ian, and it is this." I paused. "Is there any possibility that you could get over here? I mean, is it possible you could hire an ambulance to take you to the plane, even have a stretcher on board? I really think we could look after you here, better than you staying in Morocco."

He was outstandingly direct and said it in a cheerful, matter-of-fact kind of voice, as if he had decided days ago.

"Nicole, that's very sweet of you, baby, but it is over with Ellen. It is as simple as that. I haven't mentioned it to her yet, because she had her opening night, and I didn't want to distract her."

He went on as if he was discussing a business deal, rationally, without any kind of emotion.

"She has her career, which means the world to her. Our marriage was postponed because of it and so she made her choice. If she wanted to be with me then she would be. I want someone who treats me as number one, honey, I don't really feel that we could have a good life when I would be put on hold every so often, because she has to go and act somewhere. Look I needed her here, I was going to sell this place, but now I have decided not to, because I still have lots of friends here, and by the way, they are taking care of me very nicely."

I could hear voices in the background. Could they also hear what he was saying? It was a rather personal conversation, a serious one, so if they could hear it, they must be very close friends.

I was dumbstruck, even though I had my suspicions. He was talking sense in a way. It was sobering. Ellen will be devastated, because she has no suspicions at all.

"When do you plan to tell her?" I had to know.

"In a week or two, I guess. Give her time to settle into her play. She's a great gal, don't get me wrong, but when she postponed the wedding in Venice, well it got me thinking about our whole relationship. I wish her the best in life, but it was her decision."

"But don't you love her?"

"Of course I do. She's one of a kind. But, Nicole, grow up, I need someone with me, not going out every night to do some play."

Oh dear. He certainly didn't understand actresses. I looked out the window as we were talking, watching the pigeons sitting on the rail of the balcony. I wish they wouldn't do that and mess up the place. Somebody nearby must be feeding them. I was still shattered at what I was hearing.

"I don't think Ellen has any idea about any of this", I said in a quiet voice.

"I know she doesn't. I don't want her worrying about me, I'm fine. I hope she doesn't make a fuss."

"Make a fuss! Ian, she's in love with you. She will be terribly upset. She has no idea you feel this way."

"Well why don't you tell her then? I just want to be fair and not let any of this affect her work."

"Did you give her an ultimatum when she was offered this play?"

"No, because I thought I would be with her and we would be together. I did say I would be a stage-door Johnny and be with her, I must agree, but that was before I had the accident and then had time to reflect on what I really wanted out of a relationship. Nicole, honey, I've been around, and known many women, so by this time I should know what I want, don't you think?"

"All because she postponed the wedding. Is that it?" I was getting angry.

"No, as I told you, that was just the first inkling of how our future life might be. I would always come in second place to her career, and I'm sorry I'm not used to that."

I was about to lose my temper, thinking of the distress that Ellen would go through, so I thought I'd better get off the phone.

"I will try to talk to Ellen if I can, but I won't tell her what you have just told me. You have to do that. But I'll try to prepare her."

"Yes, would you do that honey? It will make it easier."

"But what have you been saying to her, when you speak on the phone? You talk practically every day, she tells me."

"Mostly about her play. A few queries about my leg. What the doctors say, what kind of meals do I have, all that stuff. It is all rather repetitive. I have held off saying anything because I know she will be upset."

"Well, bully for you!" I thought. At least he has some kind of realization of what a shock it will be for her.

"I'm sorry. I have to go now. I have to go out. I doubt if we will talk again. Goodbye."

I slammed down the phone. I couldn't believe it. I was angry and shocked. So I could well imagine how Ellen would feel. I will have to start talking to her very diplomatically, sowing seeds of suspicion about Ian, without having her so upset that she would confront him and be told the truth too soon.

I looked at the clock. Lord, it was 6.45.p.m. At least I was ready. I grabbed my coat, slammed the door and hailed a cab.

Nigel was waiting just inside the door of the restaurant. He looked fabulous. Tanned, in a well tailored suit, and incredibly handsome. He gave me his sexiest smile. I was trembling, as he kissed me on the lips. After the conversation I had just it was difficult to look him in the eye, because I was still mad at Ian and felt I hated all men at that moment. Nigel might not understand if I told him.

We sat at my favorite table and I suddenly realized that it was the exact table I had sat with Ian and Ellen. Oh dear, it was too much.

"Nigel, would you mind if we moved our table. I'd like to sit at the back, near that lovely painting of the ships."

"Not at all." He beckoned the waiter and it was quickly arranged. After we were seated and ordered drinks, I felt slightly better. Now, if I could only concentrate on Nigel and not think of Ian, I would be able to get through the meal without breaking down.

I ordered a stiff gin and tonic. He was obviously pleased to see me, and took my hand as if to say, I want you to belong to me. Oh, ho … what do I say to that?

I needn't have worried. He was so different from Ian and his conversation about Jamaica was so interesting, I began to unwind. The food was absolutely delicious, and he ordered another bottle of wine. They had no grilled onions on the menu, so I ordered them to be specially cooked. We laughed as we shared them with the steak and we both knew that we would end up in bed.

"I sold the house finally, suddenly the new owners changed their minds and wanted to move in immediately. They originally said three months, but their house sold quickly, so they had nowhere to go. I really didn't mind, but that's why I'm back so suddenly."

"What will you do now?"

He had all kinds of plans. Meetings with executives in the City, and several projects in hand.

"I think it is bad luck to talk about new ventures before they happen, don't you?" I really wanted to say that I felt it was too premature for him to me telling him about his future. He would expect me to comment and I really didn't know enough about all the things that I knew he would want to discuss. Like world trade agreements, balance of payments, the stock market, futures and all the things that City types talk about.

We went back to the Dorchester and it was a night of love-making that I will never forget. As I lay there in the morning light, I thought no matter what happens, I will have this night to remember as my 'Dorchester night'.

I looked over to Nigel, who was still sleeping on his back, memorizing his profile. He had a rather nice nose, his eyelashes were long and curly. I was very happy, even though I had no idea what was going to happen. Could I trust this man? Men seem to have a very different idea of commitment. I couldn't help thinking of Ian. Maybe it wasn't his fault that he had a totally different outlook on life, especially regarding relationships. Had he treated Ellen badly? I'm sure he thought he hadn't. In fact, he kind of indicated in his tone of voice, that she had let him down. Basically he was a nice chap who probably had no idea just how much he was going to hurt Ellen.

I wondered if Nigel could hurt me as much. Should I let him get close?

Well, darling he couldn't have been more close than last night, I smiled to myself. I kept watching his profile, waiting for him to wake up.

Finally he did, and we made love all over again.

We had breakfast brought to the room. I stayed in bed, under the sheets as the waiter with the trolley wheeled it in. Such luxury. Silver coffee service, hot toast and muffins, scrambled eggs under the silver covers, and a fresh rose in a tiny vase. I put on the hotel's terry cloth robe, and sat down to pour the coffee. We both smiled at each other, he came around to massage my neck.

It was so pleasant sitting in this room after the boredom of my own flat. No matter how nice it is, it gets boring. I thought that must buy some new prints or something, before Nigel comes over. But then, they would be new to him, I guess.

After drinking his coffee, he settled his long frame into an armchair, put his fingertips together and regarded me with a pleased expression.

"I am in love with you, Nicole. Do you know that? I think those grilled onions worked for me?" He smiled.

I didn't know what to say. I wanted to say I loved him too, but it all seemed to be too early. It was slightly embarrassing, because I didn't want to commit myself. I just didn't know enough about him. To divert the obvious answer that was expected of me, I decided to tell him about Ellen and Ian. He listened to all of it, which included telling him of the conversation with Ian last night.

"That's why I was slightly late last night. I was sorry to have kept you waiting", I explained.

"I thought you looked a little upset, I must admit."

"I was so angry with Ian. Don't you think he is being unfair?" I was curious.

He shrugged. "It's hard to say, not knowing either of them, but it does seem a little hard on Ellen."

Sometimes you learn more about a person when you hear what they think of your friends. But then he hadn't met them. But he was sympathetic towards Ellen, so that was a good sign.

We spent the day together. It was not raining for once and we walked up Park Lane and across into the park. He was pleased to be back he said, and he was eager to make plans.

It was beginning to sink in that I was in love with him too, but as I always knew about myself, I am a pushover for falling in love.

He came back to the flat with me about 6 o'clock and I fixed a chicken dinner with some new recipe I had tried out a week or so ago. Again we couldn't take out hands off each other ending up in bed. What sex. It was real chemistry. So much so, I wondered if it was the best ever. He left to go back to the hotel later on, as I was already asleep.

I'd turned off the phone earlier just in case any one called while we were love making in bed, also I knew that Ellen would call and I wanted to be able to talk to her without Nigel being there.

Next day he went to Oxford, to visit his mother. He wanted me to go with him to meet her, but I thought it was pushing it a bit. He was going to stay a week but decided he wanted to find a place to live in London as soon as possible so would return in three days.

CHAPTER 24

▼

After he had left the next morning, I tidied up the flat, emptied the dishwasher, waiting till around noon to phone Ellen. I didn't really know what to say to her, I didn't know whether to tell her that I had actually phoned Ian. It seemed very disloyal and underhand but it was up to him to tell her what he had told me. I wondered when he would choose to do this. It was not right that she should hear it from me.

He had said that he wanted to wait till she settled into the play, but I knew Ellen, she would be pushing him to return to London every time she talked to him. I had to warn her.

Finally, I called. She was cheerful and bright, telling me about some friends who had taken her out for a delicious unforgettable meal in Soho after the show last night.

"Where were you yesterday?" she asked. "You were out all day. I called lots of times, and finally gave up."

I told her all about Nigel and how much had happened since I'd last spoken to her, which was the truth.

"We ended up spending the night at the Dorchester, which was heaven."

"I'm so happy for you, Nicole. You deserve the best. But please be careful. You were lucky with having someone as decent as Peter, but there are some bastards out there, just remember Michael."

"Yes, I know." How well I know. Then I began my strategy.

"Ellen, have you ever thought that Ian might just want to stay on in Morocco? I mean, he seems to have a nice place down there even though neither of us has seen it."

She wasn't that dumb. Obviously she had been thinking about it, as he hadn't said when the doctors had told him he could travel.

"I've thought about it a lot. Especially as he hasn't been calling very much at all. In fact, I am calling more now, because I'm worried about him."

"Perhaps he does feel like he has been a second choice for you, in the fact that you chose the play and postponed the wedding." Oh dear, it was so difficult.

"Whose side are you on?" she said suspiciously.

"Yours, of course. But I hope you are not going to be mad at me, but I did talk about you to Nigel last night."

"You did? What did you say?" I felt a slight irritation in her voice.

"That you were my closest friend and if your wedding had taken place this last weekend in Venice, that I wouldn't have been in London when he called."

"Oh yes? Is that all?"

"Well, he did say that Ian must have been very disappointed."

"Not as much as I was". She sounded on edge.

"Ellen, what if Ian decides to stay in Morocco, and not come back to London? He must be missing you, so much so, that you would think he would get an ambulance and stretcher somehow and get back here. You know he is a resourceful man."

There I'd said what I wanted to say.

"I don't know. Anyway this conversation is depressing me, Nicole, I think about it all the time, but there is nothing much I can do. He has to make the move and if he doesn't then it's too bad."

Changing the subject to distract her, I asked about the play, also I wanted my observation to sink in. I had tried to warn her and didn't want to go any further, because as Ian had said, it would be better to wait till she was well into the play.

I needed to get out of the flat, just in case she called me back wanting to discuss the problem in further detail. The refrigerator was empty, or nearly empty and we had finished all the wine. So shopping was a necessity, besides I knew the exercise would make me feel better. More of everything was needed. I wanted to buy some very good wine for Nigel, I knew he was used to it and my el cheapo stuff would not do.

Peter used to buy some lovely wine, but I had never written down the names, or kept the labels. So I would have to use my own initiative. Champagne, of course, was easy, even though I only liked it occasionally.

Nigel called after I had returned and unpacked all the groceries.

"Darling, I've got some interesting news. I want you to come up here. Today I saw a house for sale, just outside Oxford which I think I might buy if you like it."

You could have blown me down with a feather. I was so surprised by the news.

"I thought you went to visit your mother?" I said.

"Yes, I'm here now. I took her out for lunch, and she suggested a short drive in the country. She's got a nice new car by the way. We were driving about five miles down from the river and there was a 'for sale' sign on a lovely old house, which actually backs on to the river. I took the telephone number, called the agent and saw the house this afternoon. It is a lovely place with modern bathroom and kitchen, the garden runs down to the river. Mother says that the price is right for that area. So it won't last long. I want you to see it. Can you come up? I know it is sudden, but I've thought about it and it makes sense. We could have a place up here and one in London."

Good heavens, I thought. Talk about sudden. I didn't know what to think. Were his next few words going to be a proposal over the phone? I was astonished and at the same time, flattered that he had already imagined us living together, married or not, that he wanted me to see the house before he bought it. I had to think quickly. If I said something like, "Oh, you don't need me there. If you like it, buy it", that might indicate that I wasn't that interested in him or the house, or that I had no intention of living there. So I said that I'd love to come and see it, which was the truth.

"There is a train tonight at 7 o'clock, which I could meet, or if you want to wait till the morning, there is one at ten." He had already checked the times before he phoned me, so I knew he was serious.

"I think it's better if I wait till the morning and then we can have a better look at the place. Besides, I'm sure your mother wants some time with you alone, on your first day back."

Did that sound all right? I wanted to sound as enthusiastic as he was, but it was still such a surprise. Like he was planning our future before I had got around to thinking about it.

What a man, I smiled, thinking of living in a country house with such a handsome bloke. I'd really been lucky meeting him in Jamaica. It was scary to think that we may have never met. Fate does have to do with everything I decided.

Some ships do pass in the night, but others stay around. Like Nigel. Why was I hesitating? Only because it seemed too good to be true.

I left a message on Ellen's machine saying I was going up to Oxford to stay a day or two with Nigel when I knew she would be at the theatre. I was chicken, but I didn't want to talk about Ian anymore. I didn't want to hasten the shock and pain that she was about to experience.

Nigel was there at the station, looking gorgeous. He had a great sense of dress. Always appropriate.

"Good morning, darling," he embraced me, then kissed me. My heart raced, he felt so warm and cuddly. I could have gone to bed right then.

"Good morning" We smiled at each other with pleasure. He had on a lovely camel hair coat,with a Burberry scarf, he took my hand, even though he still had his driving gloves on, as we walked out of the station.

"I know this is rather a surprise, but I wanted your opinion."

My opinion? I'd give him anything he wants. I was in love.

He had brought his mother's car, a Blue Mercedes and we drove down to see the house. He had already arranged with the agent for our visit. We drove down some leafy lanes, through a pretty village that had some thatched cottages, nestled around the pub on the corner, crossed an old stone bridge, then turned into a tree lined drive. It was all he said it to be and more. There in front of us was a charming old brick house, with ivy growing up the front of the house which had a yellow front door. As we went in, I saw the polished wood floors, covered with ornate rugs and a lambswool skin by the living room door. There were flag stones in the kitchen which had a large picture window looking out on to willow trees and a long lawn. A classic country house, with three bedrooms and two bathrooms.

When I heard the price, I looked at Nigel with new eyes. Was he that rich? He asked all kinds of questions which the agent knew or read off the listing. Taxes were not as high as he had thought, the roof had been recently redone and the leak in the second bedroom was now fixed.

We walked around the garden, there was a magnolia tree, under the master bedroom window. How lovely, you would be able to smell its fragrance in the summer. An apple and peach tree, more blossom in the spring and a bed of roses near the gate to the vegetable garden. Yes, I loved the place immediately. We could get a dog perhaps, a golden retriever and a cat. Suddenly I thought that a lot of people must live like this, they have houses like this, they have a dog, animals, a garden!

A garden. I hadn't had a garden since I was a kid. No matter if it seemed sort of new to me, it WAS regarded as rather normal after all. It's just that I had never really thought about it before … He put his arm around me as we went back into the house.

'Well, what do you think?" He could tell by my face, what I thought.

"It's lovely. I think you should buy it." I avoided saying "we", in case he thought I was presumptuous. It was his money after all.

"I thought you would like it. It is a little different from your city life, of course." He sat down in one of the armchairs in the den.

It turns out that the owners were living abroad. They were selling the house as is. That is, with all the furniture if we wanted it. I thought it was fine. The colour choice was perfect and most of the curtains and bedcovers looked new, as if they had never been used.

"Saves all the bother of scouting for furniture and endless trips to Dickens and Jones for curtains or whatever", I said. I hate to shop especially now that all the stores have piped in music. It is no pleasure at all.

We drove back to his mother's house. It was very similar to the one we had just left, except it was a good deal smaller. As I got out of the car, I found I was nervous and quite anxious about meeting his mother. She opened the door, and I knew immediately she was a lovely woman.

"Mother, I'd like to introduce you to Nicole. Nicole Bennett. Nicole, this is Mother."

We smiled at each other and I, being used to be kissed, wanted to kiss her, but was surprised when Nigel's mother kissed me.

"How do you do, Mrs.Fox?"

"Please don't let's be formal. Why don't you call me Nora?"

"Nora and Nicole", laughed Nigel. I like that. We went into the house where lunch was ready in the dining room,

His mother was charming and obviously adored him. I was beginning to too. It was a delicious lunch, and a maid came to take the plates away. I realized that Nora must have met Nigel's first wife, I wondered how I compared with her in Nora's eyes. Only time will tell.

They certainly had a lot to talk about. She seemed very interested in my career, but didn't know very much about what plays were on in the West End now. She talked about Noël Coward though, and had met him when she went out to visit Nigel in Jamaica.

"He was so brilliantly witty", she said. "We went to Blue Harbour several times for dinners and he always had celebrities staying with him who were great fun as well. So many laughs, and so many stories about actors and the theatre it was like watching one of his plays. Very entertaining. I was so sorry to hear about his death. The end of an era, of course. There will never be anyone like him I'm sure."

She had seen all his contemporaries too. Laurence Olivier, "his Richard the Third couldn't be matched". And Edith Evans. "Her voice was incredible", she said.

Nora's memory was remarkable: she reeled off the names and plays, as if she had seen them onstage yesterday.

"It was an era that one will always remember. The acting was so outstanding, and the performers were held in such esteem. You knew that you were seeing great theatre and it is a shame that more of it wasn't filmed", she said.

I went on to say that it is very difficult to capture the magic of a stage performance on film. It has to do with that particular bond between the actors on stage with a live audience. It is like a live, pulsing force, a communication that is living at that precise moment and cannot be captured on film.

After lunch, Nigel and I went over to the agent's office and he signed papers and cheques to secure the offer for the house. It was very sudden, too sudden really to make sense, but I suppose if you know you want something, like this house, you had to move. No procrastinating. I watched Nigel conduct business. It was astounding, I learnt a lot.

Would he become bored with me, I wondered. I had so little experience of these kind of things, and for the first time could see how men operate when they are doing business.

Next, he would turn his focus on me, I thought, and ask me what I wanted to do. It was all a bit soon, a bit sudden, but I felt confident that we would get on very well together. I wanted all the things he wanted.

We went on to a pub to celebrate because as he said, he felt as if he had offered enough that he would get the house. He wanted me to stay over with him. His mother had some business he had to attend to, also he had some contacts he had to follow up about finding work in the City. I hadn't brought more than a change of clothes so felt I needed to go home and think things out too. Although he hadn't mentioned marriage I knew that would be the next thing on his agenda. I needed time to think.

He took me to the station and kissed me on the lips with his hand pushing my lower back into him. Sexy beast. He was such an animal. I was sorry to be leaving, but thought it would be slightly embarrassing to sleep over anyway in his mother's house. She may think that it would be rather common to do that.

The train was delayed about an hour on the track. Oh dear, will we have to put up with this, if we live out there. I would have to get a car rather than take the train.

By the time I got in it was well past nine. There were four messages on the phone ... all from Ellen. The worst had happened. Ian had told her obviously, he must have told her he wasn't coming back, because she sounded distraught.

I went to bed, thinking what a pleasant day I had had and there was a new world out there for me whereas Ellen's world had been shattered. I wondered what she would do.

CHAPTER 25

▼

Since I had returned from New York, I was curious to know why I hadn't heard from Dianne. I had sent her a thank you note to say how much I had enjoyed the voyage and would love to do it again sometimes in the future. Then I remembered she was down in Florida, setting up her new office with a warehouse, buying books by the yard. I would have to wait until she got back although I wanted to talk to her.

I thought of calling her, because I wanted to see if she still wanted me to contact actors to perform on board and maybe do another show myself. It would be such a different kind of occupation, and something that appealed to me.

It was comforting to think that there was other work I could do which was close to providing stimulus and pleasure to people. Musicians have music, artists create, I believe, not only to paint for themselves but for other people. If they don't communicate their idea or inspiration on the canvas, then I think they have failed. But then I never liked modern art and I think the real reason that that millionaire gave so many Picassos to the Museum, besides tax reasons, was because he couldn't stand looking at them any longer at home!

I felt that bringing books, actors, and the sea together was a great idea and I couldn't thank Dianne enough to be part of her life. She would be up to her ears in work so I resisted calling her and thought it best to wait for her call.

In the meantime, it was the usual calls from Tony to do some work either in the wilds of Scotland, or Canada or Australia. The parts weren't good enough. I had played most of them before and I wasn't go to trek out to Ontario to do Stratford there. Besides they had perfectly good Canadian actors who needed the work. Perhaps they had needed the British stars when they first opened there, but they had been such a success, they could now attract their own audiences.

I waited for Ellen's call. I was right. After questioning Ian rather forcefully, he obviously decided he must say something now, rather than wait any longer. He broke the news that he had decided to stay in Morocco. Of course, I knew she would be inconsolable, but I didn't expect her reaction to be so angry.

"Nicole, I'm going to shoot him. I'm so angry, I'm really going to kill him. I will take Sunday through Tuesday. Monday we are off, as you know. I will fly out there and kill him and if I can't do it, I'll get some creepy Moroccan gypsy to kill him."

Hell hath no fury, but this was going much too far.

"I loved him and now I hate him. He is a total bastard. How could he just say that he is now just second to my career, when he encouraged me to take the job-saying how proud of me he was, and how he would come to the theatre every night!"

I waited her out. She went on in a rage. All the usual things about lack of honesty, lying and most of all that he seemed to have had a woman in the background out there all the time he had known her.

"I have to do this Nicole, I won't rest till he is dead and can't do this kind of thing to any other woman."

I looked out the window and the pigeons were there again. How simple a bird's life is, I thought, none of this sturm and drang. Do they cheat on each other? I wondered.

"Nicole, don't you tell anyone. I shouldn't have told you, I wasn't going to, but I need to tell someone and I trust you even though you don't seem to understand."

"Of course I understand. We have both been there. Most women have, but they don't go round killing the bastard."

"Some do," she said.

"You will be caught and then you will go to jail," I stated very calmly. "It might even be in a Moroccan jail, which would be terrible. Think of the misery and hell of that … would it be worth it? He's not worth all that horror you would have to endure afterwards. He would be dead after all so he wouldn't feel a thing. You would be suffering far worse than you are now, believe me. They may even execute you. He's not worth it."

"But I won't be caught. I will do it so no one will know."

"Do you even know where to get a gun?" I couldn't help smiling to myself. This is ridiculous. It is so crazy maybe I should just let her rampage away until she sees sense.

The thought of a Moroccan jail did actually calm her down. If she had to hire someone she didn't know she probably couldn't trust them, even if she paid a great deal of money.

I didn't know if she was having a breakdown but I felt immediate concern that she might not get to the theatre on time. She was also taking tranquilizers and I knew she had been drinking, it was just possible she might not make it.

"Look here, I'm coming round to see you. You are no condition to come over here. Do you need food? Go and look in the fridge and tell me. No, don't bother, I'll pick up some food on the way. At least then I'd know she had something to eat."

She was in a terrible state when I got there. She looked dreadful and kept crying and punching the cushion on the sofa.

"He was so cool, and unemotional, as if he was talking about a business deal", she wept.

I knew what she meant. He'd been the same way when talking to me.

"How can you misjudge a person so badly? I trusted him, he was so very trustworthy. That's what I liked about him, he wasn't like other men. He was mature and level headed."

Her whole body was contorted up. She kept hugging herself, pulling at her hair., covering her mouth with her hands. She was absolutely devastated. Walking up and down when she wasn't punching cushions, almost wringing her hands as a Greek woman would. I thought perhaps I should call the theatre. How could she possibly work tonight?

Under all this, I was listening to her words, which echoed all my nervousness about my own new lover. I would never want to go through the agony of two years ago, or what Ellen was going through now, and yet here I was falling in love with a man I didn't know very well at all.

I went into the bathroom and soaked a hand towel in cold water and brought it to her.

"Look at your face Ellen, you've got to stop crying. You are all swollen and make-up is not going to cover it tonight if you don't stop now. Scream if you like, but don't cry."

Eventually I made her sit down in her kitchen and eat some scrambled eggs. Lots of coffee and some of her favorite ice-cream which I remembered to pick up when shopping.

We sat there looking at each other, eyeball to eyeball. She was still in shock and couldn't believe all this was happening.

"If I'd only known he would feel like this, I would never had taken the job", she whispered.

"Listen, if it wasn't now it would have been later. Better it was now, than later." I had to say something to comfort her, although it wasn't much.

I still thought she just might go out there and try to buy a gun she looked so distraught. 'Over my dead body', I thought.

But Dr. Theatre came to the rescue. As soon as you go onstage, in front of footlights, your body and its ailments, disappear like magic, it's a well known fact. So, I managed to get her to the theatre, and stayed with her even though her dresser wasn't pleased. She pulled herself together as the old pro that she was, and gave a wonderful performance as I watched out front.

Later I took her home and put her to bed. I stayed till she was asleep, which was well after midnight and thought she would be out of it until early morning.

When I got home, there were two messages from Nigel. It was too late to call him, but I wondered what was up.

CHAPTER 26

▼

I waited till 8 o'clock next morning to call him even though I knew that he probably would have been up for hours. I already missed hearing his voice. It must be love I thought. Yes, I was in love with him. I had fallen in love with him I was sure. Oh dear, here I go again, I knew it would happen if I went to bed with him. Honestly it's really pathetic in this day and age.

His mother answered the phone. "Good morning Nicole, how are you? I hope you your trip was pleasant."

I told her about the delay.

'Well that doesn't often happen. Just minute and I'll find Nigel."

I heard her calling him. He must have been outside in the garden.

She came back to the phone. "He's just coming. It was so nice to meet you yesterday, Nicole. I enjoyed our conversation about the theatre tremendously!"

I thanked her for the lunch and her hospitality and was almost going to say, and thanks for giving birth to Nigel, but I thought it might sound cheeky.

I would have to be careful not to upset her, as I knew how much she admired him. I hoped he wasn't a 'mother's boy', who would run back to her if we had a fight. Not to worry, I thought, I'll soon find out.

"Hullo, darling. Good morning. How are you?" Once again that voice was heaven. So warm and well spoken.

"I'm fine. How are you?" I felt happy listening to him.

"Great. It looks as it we have the house. They made a counter offer, but the agent said he thinks they will take my second offer."

"That's wonderful. When will you know?"

"Probably today, sometime."

- 155 -

"Please call me and let me know, won't you?"

"Of course. I tried to call last night but you were out."

"Yes, it was a stressful evening, after such a lovely day with you."

I told him about Ian's phone call and Ellen's reaction to it, how I had to go over and calm her down, and get her to and from the theatre.

"She was a basket case, I was very worried about her. I hope she has recovered today. I'll call her later and see how she is."

"Let's hope she hasn't gone off to Morocco", he said.

"I talked her out of that, I think."

I wanted to know if he was returning today and if he was going to stay here with me. I wanted him to, but I felt slightly uncomfortable about it and he too seemed rather awkward about it, as if he felt he was intruding slightly, and I sensed that he wanted to stay with his mother a little longer.

"There is a lot to be done really. I have to buy a car, settle up the rest of the Jamaican paper work, get my portfolio together, it really will take quite some time.

I was very tempted, but I still worried about Ellen, she was so upset that I felt I had to be around for her. Who knows, she maybe crazy enough to take off for Morocco.

Joan called about ten minutes after Nigel. She wanted to know if I would go with her to the hearing tomorrow morning. Even though the lawyers would be there, she needed some one else to be with her. I said of course I would go even though I knew it that it would be such a grim experience. She was so anxious. The laywers had done all they could.

Next morning was an eye opener. I had never been in a court room before, so I didn't know who was who, which lawyer was which, or how things were conducted. I just sat and listened.

Then, suddenly, Charlotte's lawyer came in, and beckoned us to come outside. As the tension was so great, I was pleased to be out of there.

The other lawyer, who had been brought in to help with the case, was there outside waiting for us. He asked us all to sit down. Charlotte and Joan looked terrible as if they hadn't slept all night, which they probably hadn't.

The time was just about now that they would be asking for Charlotte, in the court room to deliver the verdict. It didn't look good. I couldn't imagine how anyone could send her to jail. But these things happen I know.

"I think we have now got information that will throw the case out of court", said the lawyer. He pulled some papers out of his briefcase. Then he told us the news.

"Evidently the police made an error in the spelling of this guy's name. I had his name checked out on old files. His name is spelt incorrectly on this file. When I finally found the correct spelling of his name, and looked him up he seems as if he has been charged three times for this same offence and has already been fined heavily."

Charlotte broke down in tears with relief and Joan looked at the lawyer as if he was a genius.

"That's unbelievable", she said.

We were all dumbfounded. A simple spelling mistake.

I immediately wondered if the police woman had anything to do with the mistake. Surely she wouldn't want to let this man off, and send Charlotte to jail?

We were all very complimentary to the lawyer and congratulated both of them on such brilliant work. It was such a hair's breath away from an absolute disaster, it was scary to think of it. How terrible it could have been and would have been if they hadn't got the second lawyer to help.

We all went back into the court room and we watched as the lawyers reported this news and watched the proceedings with great interest. The police woman had to acknowledge the mistake and the man admitted he had been caught before. The evidence was all there. The guy got fined again and was allowed to go home. It didn't seem to matter to anyone, including the police, that he was free the do the same thing all over again, although this time they may not misspell his name.

CHAPTER 27

▼

Well it's over. My idea of working with Dianne. I just phoned Miami and got through to her office. She died last week. She had developed melanoma and by the time they found it was too late. She had been so busy building her business she hadn't seen a doctor in years. I couldn't believe it.

I still can't believe it. The shocking thing is that she was caring for a close friend of hers who had breast cancer and used to sit with her during her chemotherapy treatments. Being so attentive to her that she hadn't even noticed the lump between her shoulders blades and another one on the back of her neck.

It is appalling that someone can be so fatally ill and not know it. The news was as devastating as hearing that a member of the family had died. She had helped so many people, giving jobs to dozens of her friends and family. She trained and gave jobs to both men and women who became librarians on the ships and travelled the world. She worked so hard choosing and ordering hundreds of books from book lists from best sellers, to the classics, from biographies to naval history. Cataloguing them and updating them constantly for all the libraries.

From just one library, to dozens, she had amassed a small empire and with it some very loyal friends. Why is it that the good die young? Why is it that so many of them are taken from us.

The phone rang again. For distraction I answered it. It was Jane. She made me feel better because she wanted to tell me how grateful she was for all I had done for her.

"If you hadn't stopped to talk to me that day, I don't know what would have happened. You really saved my life, by introducing me to Beryl. I have bought you a little gift and I wonder if we could meet so I can give it to you. Or if you are passing the theatre anytime, I'm usually there by 7.30 at half time."

I'd forgotten that she was in the play every night, of course.

"Well, you certainly didn't have to buy me anything you know that. I am sure that Beryl is grateful to have you."

Then Joan called to thank me for going to the court house, and being so supportive. So at least I was trying to do my bit but nothing like the work of Dianne. She will be missed terribly. Everyone who knew her will feel the loss. I had never known anyone like her. The whole idea that she was gone filled me with terrible sadness. She was such an inspiration, and she seemed to know how to help her friends. To help find a way to discover what was inside them and what they could do to express themselves, either through work, or by changing their personal lives. Everybody I spoke to, who knew her, said the same thing. She helped all of us, we all agreed.

The reason was because she seemed to know so many important people and she would use her contacts freely, to help someone get ahead. Everybody liked her, so she could ask any of these influential people to grant her request. Getting a world famous conductor to engage a brilliant but unknown concert pianist, for example, which lead him to a recording contract. I heard of dozens of stories like that from her friends later.

I remember her plans for more book outlets. She spoke of a library for the Orient Express for example, just one of the other places she thought of, and now all future plans had vanished into thin air.

Nigel called and I told him the news. He was sympathetic, but never having met her, it was difficult for him to know what she meant to me.

It's like that person you know who you feel will always be there for you, someone who you know is one of the best people on earth, they can't help it they are just there for you. A real friend, someone you admire. They give of themselves effortlessly wherever they go. They are naturals and have the gift of making your life happier without realizing it, it just happens.

These people are the real angels on earth, and she was one of them. I've known two or three in my life and it is sad to think that perhaps there are some of us who have never met one of them.

Ellen was the next one to call, but I wasn't up to talking for long. She had calmed down but not much. This is something that she knew she would have to solve with Ian. She thanked me for getting her through the worst part of the shock, and forcing to go to the theatre that night.

I told her about Dianne's death, but again, like Nigel she had never met her but knew how much she had meant to me. I think it stopped her going on too much about her own problem, as she knew I was suffering too, in a different way. I told her of the great loss and that I wondered if I would ever meet another person quite like her. One who had opened up a whole new world to me, literally new horizons, like performing on huge ocean liners for example, and meeting people like ship's captains, or famous opera singers, or concert pianists. People who have outstanding international lives and experiences, who become friends and therefore broaden one's own day to day life, with their friendship.

CHAPTER 28

▼

Why is it when you least expect something to happen, when you are thinking about other things entirely, and you have decided that nothing is as you expect things ... it does.

Tony called with a great offer. To play Cleopatra in New York. It was one role I had always wanted to play and when the Shakespeare Memorial Theatre did it three years ago I wanted to do it then, but was working in Los Angeles.

I was very pleased when he called. It is always nice to feel someone wants you for a certain role. That your name has obviously been discussed and then they call your agent.

It had been a long time since I had been in New York to work.

"It is a six month contract. But rehearsals start here for a month beforehand. You have two days to make up your mind as I said you were out of town otherwise they would have expected an answer immediately. Now, Nicole, be a good girl and don't mess me about."

"Thank you Tony. I will need at least two days."

He told me the terms, the billing order and the other names who had been contacted for the leads.

"Who do they want for Mark Anthony?" I was eager to know.

"They wouldn't tell me as he hasn't signed yet."

"But I must know that, of course."

"Of course. Maybe I'll find out tomorrow."

After the initial pleasure of such an offer had worn off and I had recovered from the rush of adrenalin, I went into the kitchen, made coffee and sat down to think it through.

"Here we go again", I thought. At least Michael is out of the picture now, and poor dear Peter. But what to do about Nigel? We are talking about my personal life again and which is more important. I wish I had a mentor to advise me. But I knew what they would say. Which is more important? No use asking Ellen.

I was very excited about playing that great role. It is such a fantastic part. It was exactly what I would choose for myself at the moment if anyone had asked me.

What will I say to Nigel?

I phoned Joan to ask her advice. She had met Nigel and knew how I felt about him. She couldn't help at all.

"It's your decision Nicole. Whatever you do, make up your mind that it is the best decision. You are the only one who can decide."

I phoned Beryl. She said the same thing. Honestly, what a friends for? I suppose I wanted to contradict them if they offered any advice. But they didn't. I knew I was just using them as a sounding board. Then I can talk till I'm blue in the face, and they still won't say anything.

I knew it would be the hardest decision of my life. If I turned this down, then they would think that I was no longer up for parts, that I must have retired.

Then suddenly I remembered. It came to me in a flash.

I thought of Rosemary Gibson, a wonderful actress who after having a baby two years ago, she turned down everything to give her child a good start in life. She was determined to stay home and she gave up some wonderful roles. That bond was the most important thing in her life.

So perhaps the situation didn't have to be so black and white, there must be a way, some kind of leverage. I thought about it all day and almost all night. It was becoming clearer to me. Finally I had a break through, and in actual fact, it was the only solution. Had I known this beforehand, I would have advised Ellen to do the same. But I hadn't known, so now it was too late.

I would take a break and be like Rosemary and bow out for a long break. Nigel was too important to me, too important to lose. I wasn't going to make the same mistake again as I did with Michael, when I went to Los Angeles and lost him.

It took hours to come to that decision. I suppose many actors and actresses have the freedom to take a break. Perhaps I will never be offered the part of Cleopatra again, but that was a risk I'd had to take.

When Nigel called, I told him the news, but followed quickly by saying that I had decided not to take the role and nor go to New York.

"I want to be with you, and I can always go back to work once we have established a home together."

"Darling, I don't want to stop you", he said. I knew he meant it but I wasn't going to take the risk.

"I hope you won't regret it. You must be very sure before you decide. However, I do have some good news for you. The house is ours! The sale went through."

"Oh, Nigel, that's wonderful! I'm sorry, I was so full of my news you didn't have a chance to tell me yours."

"I am delighted and I hope you are too. It will be a first home for us together. Are you pleased?"

"Absolutely! We can live here when we are in London and up there when we want to. It is great news. I'm thrilled with the house."

We made plans for the weekend. As I put down the phone, the thought came to me that he was my Mark Anthony and I was his Cleopatra. We would work out the details later.

No matter what the future held for me, I had learnt my lesson from past experience. The University of Life was the one I should have attended five years ago and it wasn't going to bother me now that I was about to take the train to Oxford. New York would have to wait.

Sitting on the damp grass in that little churchyard, looking up at the elegant church spire, I couldn't help thinking of the day we all went to the church in Jamaica, just after Brian died. He never went to church and neither did Noël Coward for that matter. They were not church-goers except for weddings and funerals, which is another reason to marvel at Coward's genius as it WAS obviously God given. Charlotte wanted to go with her grandmother to see the little church, down the road, in Port Maria where Ian Fleming, the originator of James Bond was married. It was a small church and as the bride recorded, both of them had to avert their heads from the Vicar's breath during the ceremony. Coward quickly tied old shoes on the car bumper only to find when they had driven off, that he'd tied them to his own car. We all went to the tiny church with Charlotte that day and tried to imagine the simple wedding ceremony in the old ice-cold dank dark stone chapel for the man who had, quite possibly, been scribbling sentences on a yellow legal pad that very morning, such as "he liked his martinis stirred not shaken."

The pointlessness of Brian's death was so profoundly stupid it made one sit up and think. But then if he told Beryl that he faked orgasms and expected her to believe him, well you just don't know, do you? We all go through the anguish of not being able to create masterpieces, or to invent brilliant theories, or write great masterpieces, even to make any kind of difference at all in this world, but who really carries this fact to such a degree that you would commit suicide rather than accept the fact.

I know Brian, like so many other admirers, adored Coward's work but who would become so depressed on seeing all of us there and being more successful than he was, but Brian. Normally we don't delve into bitter soul searching unless we have suddenly been faced with an enormous shock, either a loved one's death or being rejected by a publisher, then we tend to brood a lot as well as drink a lot.

Brian had wanted fame so much but he couldn't accept the fact that he didn't have the talent, or the connections to be successful. Both have to be there at a very early age. Ambition helps, but for him it just led to frustration. There was no one out there to help him.

Charlotte had a chance as she had the connections and the luck. Joan would always be there for her which for a young girl is the one thing that would help her, perhaps more than a husband who would have his own agenda, and career.

I wondered if I should leave my spot by the gravestone and go and have a drink.

I have never really been able to convey Brian's anguish to Nigel. He just didn't understand his despair. It was like trying to tell someone who had never been moved by a piece of music or work of art that music and art were important, as important as the latest news or where the economy was headed. He really wanted to inspire people, like Coward did, to be able to bring enjoyment to their lives even if it was superficial and about shallow people. The enjoyment that Coward still brings to millions of people around the world, is still there, particularly with his songs. 'A Room with a View' is certainly not for shallow people, or 'I'll See You Again'. I guess if Brian had found a bright young therapist, they might have saved him.

Walking down the road towards the pub, I felt as if he was with me. Who knows. All the characters I had met at Blue Harbour were inspiring, they had become part of my life and what happened to them is important to me. This is not just because they admired Coward and his life, but because they had become like family to me and would be my friends for the rest of my life. They too believed in "Rise above it, get on with it, life goes on." I had changed. Now, for the first time I seemed to be more concerned with my closest friends rather than my career. For the first time, my private life was now filled at last with a wonderful cast of characters which nourished me and filled the empty places in my soul.

There used to be a time when I felt awkward going into a pub by myself for a drink. Nowadays it is quite acceptable, besides it was lunch time, so everybody will be ordering food. How did I pick that pub, of all places? It was cozy inside, with horse brasses surrounding the fireplace, a beamed ceiling, old wooden tables and chairs, and an old brass warming pan hanging from the wall, a ray of sunlight from the leaded window, reflected on it, making it shine.

I phoned Nigel at last, and told him that I was not going to New York, that I wanted to get married and be with him. It took the Cornish air to bring me to my senses and immediately I had made the phone call, my feelings of a nervous breakdown passed into thin air. I would get paid, things would be resolved, it was only a matter of time.

As I entered the pub, I looked over and I saw that I was recognized by a guy from Los Angeles who turned out to be a movie scout, on vacation. We shared a table and I told him the reason I hadn't done another film, was because I hadn't found a good script. Suddenly the cuckoo in a cuckoo clock just above us, announced the time, as if on cue.

The following year Ellen, Joan, Charlotte and I were cast in a feature film, the screenplay being based on Brian's play. The title had not been changed, the film script followed his play. We were all delighted, and made sure Brian's name was the first up on the screen. I had stayed with Nigel when he needed me, I had learnt that his love was more important than playing Cleopatra that year. I had learnt that he needed me and at last I had changed enough to try to be an angel to someone else, rather than to lose him. Maybe my little shell had helped.

Tomorrow is another day, and Coward was right. Why does the show have to go on.

978-0-595-69335-1
0-595-69335-0

Printed in the United States
83820LV00004B/29/A

9 780595 693351